BLOOD MATE

HIGH HOUSE CANIS BOOK TWO

RILEY STORM

BLOOD MATE

HIGH HOUSE CANIS BOOK TWO

CHAPTER 1

"Tell me this isn't a trap."

Lucien spared him a glance. "Now Chief, why would you ask me to do something like that? You know I'm not big on promises."

Chief frowned unhappily. He didn't like that tone. "You certainly seemed confident about it back at the farm. Back when you convinced me to come along."

The leader of their welcome party smiled. "Of course I did. How else do you think I was going to get you to come out here?"

"I don't know. Sell me on the weather and the scenic views?" Chief muttered sarcastically, brushing his face clear of water. It didn't matter, because more was constantly splattering down on him.

They crouched in the wet undergrowth as a spring rainstorm raged overhead. There was little in the way of thunder or lightning, but the skies were making up for that with thick, juicy raindrops that had started falling an hour ago and hadn't let up since. The storm had settled over the little town of Plymouth Falls and the outlying areas such as where the wolf shifters waited, and it wasn't going anywhere.

Neither are we, Chief thought, shifting back and forth to keep himself loose as possible. They had been waiting in the bushes off the side of the only close road for forty-minutes. Everyone was soaked to the bone by now and thoroughly miserable, but they weren't complaining.

Not much, at least.

"Now, now, Chief," Lucien said, giving his shoulder a squeeze. "You know as well as I do, that we had to come, even it was a trap. We had no choice but to believe it was for real."

He nodded glumly. "I know. Trust me, I know. But listen man, I'm getting old. My joints creak. I'm pretty sure I have arthritis. Sitting out here in the cold and damp like this, I'm going to catch a cold. Tell me, are *you* going to bring me chicken noodle soup to feel better once we get back?"

Lucien snorted softly. "Not on your life. Find a woman to do that for you."

Chief soured, looking up through the brush at the road, trying to let the last comment roll off him.

"Shit, I'm sorry Chief. That was uncalled for." Lucien's hand returned to his shoulde,r giving it a gentler, more apologetic squeeze this time.

"Don't worry about it," he said gruffly. "I don't."

Lucien stiffened, like he was about to say something, but then didn't. Chief was glad. The last thing he wanted was to have a conversation about it out here where they were waiting.

The thing that bothered him, was the truth of it all. Chief *was* old, at least compared to most of the shifters he associated with. In his mid-forties, he wasn't particularly old, and could expect to keep up with the pack for another three decades or so before old age began to catch up with him. Benefits of being a wolf shifter, he supposed.

Of course, an elongated lifespan wasn't anything to brag about if you spent it alone. Wolves were all about the pack, and all about their mates. Chief had one, but never the other. He wanted to, but—

"Anyone hear that?" one of the other members of their party asked.

Chief's head came up as he heard what Linden was referring to. The sound of an internal combustion engine as it revved louder, bringing the vehicle and its occupants closer to the waiting shifters.

"Sounds like a trap," Chief muttered.

"Maybe, but we have to check it out anyway," Lucien reminded him, and by extension the rest of the shifters. "If it isn't, we need all the help we can get."

Chief nodded. It was true. In the six weeks since their pack of rebellious wolf shifters had moved out of the city to their secret farm house, they had done little but consolidate their numbers. Any overt action against the Tyrant-King and the rest of House Canis that they were rebelling against had been firmly and unarguably put on the back burner.

This was the closest they had come since. Word had reached them that a handful of shifters inside Moonshadow Manor, the ancestral home of the wolf shifters of House canis, were ready to flee, to take their chances at making a run for it.

"What are the odds they make it?" he asked. "Assuming this isn't a trap and the Tyrant-King isn't about to jump out of the bushes behind Linden there and say 'boo!'." He grinned as the named shifter started to look over his shoulder before catching himself and glaring.

"Slim," Lucien admitted. "But that's why we're here. To help them escape any pursuit they picked up when fleeing the Manor. We don't know their preparations. Maybe they bribed a member of the Guard to let them through."

Chief thought that unlikely. Most of the Wolf Guard who remained were fanatically loyal to the Tyrant-King, and unlikely to let themselves be bribed. They had locked down the acres of land surrounding the Manor like a fortress, not letting anyone in or our without express orders from their King.

If, and Chief believed it to be a big *if*, the shifters they were here to meet even made it off the property, there was no chance they wouldn't be pursued when they met up with he and his team. Which is why a full eight of them waited in the bushes, nearly a third of their entire strength, committed to one operation. If things went south…

"Relax," Lucien assured him as the car came closer. "We're ready for anything."

Chief didn't have time to protest, because just then the first vehicle crested the nearby hill, its headlights bouncing wildly in the dim early-evening light that was making its way through the light gray clouds. Moments later another vehicle came following it, the two colliding in a screech of metal as the pursuer tried to spin out the lead SUV.

"Everyone ready," Lucien hissed, and the shifters came

alive. This was where they had agreed to meet. A particularly deep little ravine that hid any occupants—metal or flesh alike —from being seen by anyone around them. If they needed to shift into their other forms, nobody would see them here.

The escaping vehicle, a gray SUV, bounced again as the driver took it down the shoulder of the road and then back up again as they closed on the rebels position.

"Almost."

A third vehicle careened over the top of the hill and descended into the ravine, accelerating madly to catch up. Chief noted it was already scratched and scraped. Clearly the chase had been close for some time now.

The fleeing shifters slammed on the brakes as they reached the predetermined area and a trio of them jumped out.

"Over here!" Lucien barked, standing up and waving, his head and arm visible above the brush.

The three arrowed in on the sound of his voice as one. Behind them, the gray SUV and its white companion bounced off the road and tried to run the shifters down, but the forty or so feet of cleared land wasn't smooth. The first ran into a tree trunk hidden by a bush, and the second hit a huge hole and blew out an entire axle.

Chief tensed as shifters piled out of both vehicles almost immediately, keeping up the pursuit. He counted ten in total. Ten against the eight rebels. It would be close. Though if the fleeing trio jumped in, they should win. After all, it didn't look like any of the loyalists had noticed Lucien yet, not since he'd ducked back down.

"Ready," Lucien said, and the rebels bounced slightly,

limbering up as the distance closed in a flash, the shifters moving faster than any human to close the gap.

"Now!"

Chief was launching himself forward before Lucien was finished shouting, his shoulder spearing an unsuspecting shifter in the stomach. The man grunted in surprise, his arms and legs flying forward for a moment before the momentum change caught up with them and nearly snapped them as they flew back with the rest of his body.

All around him there were thuds, cries of pain and surprise as the two sides met with thunderous impact. None of the loyalists had been expecting the attack, but they were all highly trained, and most of them reacted with reflexes that would have left a human slackjawed with shock.

Throwing himself to the side, Chief narrowly avoided a punch from one of the two attackers that hadn't gone down in the initial surprise assault. He had to back up quickly as the man came on in a flurry of blows designed to keep him off balance.

Another shape hit him from the side as Lucien took the man to the ground, slamming both hands into his face. Chief noted the attack. Ever since his mate had been threatened by the loyalists, Lucien had lost much of his compunction for hurting them. He was one of their fiercest fighters now as he realized not only his strength, but also his dedication to the cause.

Chief rushed forward, ripping a shifter he didn't recognize off the back of one of his men, sending him tumbling deeper into the bush, where his head hit a tree with a solid *thwack*.

The battle raged around him. The rebels, with the advantage of surprise, seemed to be winning. Chief looked around, trying to spot the trio they'd come to rescue. *If those jerks are just going to let us fight it out for them, then I —*

The thought died as the three came back out of the bush and engaged in the fight. But his expression changed when he saw their first target. Linden. One of *his* men.

"Trap!" he bellowed. "It's a trap!"

The others echoed his call as they fought on, but the odds had swiftly turned against them. The rebels were now outnumbered by nearly half a dozen, though several from both sides were down and unconscious. Slowly but surely the loyalists backed the remaining handful into a circle. Not one of them was unbloodied by that point.

"I sure hope your backup plan had something like this in mind," Chief muttered as Lucien appeared on his left, bleeding heavily from a cut above his right eye.

"Something like this," Lucien agreed. "Delay them for a moment, will you?"

"That's enough. Stop this!" a voice barked as one of the loyalists stepped forward. A fierce-looking man with a razor-sharp military crew cut, and a smile that was more leer than grin, gestured at the rebels who remained on their feet. "Surrender now, and no more of you shall be harmed."

"Masterful plan," Chief drawled. He'd always been the talker of the group. "I take it this was your idea?"

Twin orbs, steely in nature, focused on him, before the lips parted in a toothy smile that wasn't particularly friendly. "Yes. Yes it was. And you idiots fell for it completely."

Chief tapped his jaw. "Did we?"

The shifter—Chief didn't recognize him, which meant the Tyrant-King must have brought him in from another location recently—smiled broadly and sketched a mock bow. "Yes, you did. Thank you for proving our King right in appointing me as his Knight."

Mutters of anger went up through the rebels. The position of Knight in the House was one of great honor. The right hand of the King or Queen, the Knight was the heir to the throne upon death or retirement. That wasn't where their anger came from, however unfit for the position he may be.

The rebels were angry because the *true* Knight of House Canis was their leader, Logan Canis, and it irked them to know the Tyrant-King had already filled the position with this usurper.

"That's good enough, Chief," Lucien muttered just loud enough for the false Knight to hear.

"What? What's good enough?"

"His stalling job," Lucien said cheerfully. "You see, we've moved a little too far away from our original position. They had to move to find a better sightline."

"What? Who had to move? What are you talking about?"

The answer became evident a moment later as two of the loyalists when down, roaring in pain. A moment later, two more spun around as slugs impacted upon them. A fifth was hit in the back and sprawled forward between Lucien and Chief, who both stepped away as the skin on his back turned black and writhed.

"Some backup plan," Chief muttered, but he was already hauling ass.

The rebels picked up their wounded and disappeared back into the forest. A moment later two more rebels appeared, both of them with sighted rifles pulled into their shoulders, backing up slowly as they covered the escape.

"This isn't going to go over well with anyone," Chief muttered as they reached their vehicles, still hidden on a nearby service road. "That's a major escalation."

Lucien shot him a glare as they hopped in the front seat of a black pickup together. "Would you rather I let them take us all in?" he snapped.

"Of course not. But uranium weapons? Nobody has resorted to that yet. Now you've opened a can of worms."

"I know," Lucien hissed, obviously angry at himself. "But I had no choice. Logan and I both agreed that we couldn't risk any more of our strength if it was a trap."

Chief nodded as the truck rumbled to life. He understood. But uranium-filled bullets were a brutal way to escalate the civil war raging between various factions of House Canis. The radiation the uranium contained played hell with shifter DNA, breaking it apart at a cellular level and killing it off.

Hence the blackened, dead flesh on the shifter that had gone face-first in the dirt near them. One bullet wasn't enough to kill unless it was a headshot, but the five or so shifters who had been hit would be in considerable pain and agony for several days.

"Besides," Lucien growled. "They started this."

Chief then remembered that Lucien had been stabbed with a uranium-tipped dagger almost two months ago, and had nearly bled out seeking help. He would have no sympathy for the loyalists.

"Right."

The radio crackled to life and Lucien grabbed it as they headed down the service road, the other truck following behind.

"It was a trap," he said angrily. "Had to go with the backup plan."

"Shit." Logan's voice came over the other side. "That's no good. Everyone make it out?"

Chief nodded. He'd done a count as they ran. Everyone had made it out, though some of them would require a few days to heal up. Linden in particular had had a rough go of it.

"Yeah, we're all on our way home, once we've made sure we aren't being followed," Lucien said into the black radio speaker.

"Good." There was a pause, a crackle of static. "Chief there with you?"

Chief sat up straighter. Why was Logan asking for him?

"Yes," Lucien said slowly, also confused. "He's right here next to me."

"Good," Logan snapped. "Chief. Get your ass back here on the double. I'm tired of dealing with your problem for you."

Chief's eyebrows were practically merging with his hairline by this point. Lucien gave an affirmative and the radio went silent. Slowly he lifted his gaze to Lucien.

"What the hell is he talking about?"

CHAPTER 2

It was with more than a bit of trepidation that Chief watched the farmhouse grow in the distance.

After they had fled the trap, the two trucks had taken separate, circuitous routes back to their base of operations to ensure they weren't followed. The long drive through countryside and outskirts of town had ground away at his nerves until there was practically nothing left. Chief was on edge, raw and exposed.

Logan hadn't contacted them, again, and if he wasn't willing to tell Chief what was going on the first time, it was unlikely he'd be willing to do so at all. This was something he had to handle in person. Whatever it was.

"I still don't know what problem of mine he could be talking about," Chief muttered. "I don't *have* any problems. Not that would affect him, at least," he added to stave off any smart-assed remarks from the other occupants of the truck. "He sounded serious too, didn't he?"

Lucien nodded. "Yeah. He knows that this mission wasn't easy on the nerves. He wouldn't mess with you as a prank. Not right now."

"That's what scares me," Chief admitted. "I have literally no idea what this could be about. I don't have anything I've been hiding that could have exploded in his face while I'm gone."

The others just shrugged and shifted uncomfortably. They were tired of hearing him try to puzzle it out, but Chief didn't really care. He was beyond confused at this point.

Lucien headed straight for the big ranch-style house that served as their headquarters, parking next to one of the other trucks around the side, out of sight of the driveway. The others piled out and headed for one of the barns, interested in rest and food, leaving Chief alone to face the issue himself.

"Here goes nothing," he muttered, striding across the driveway, nearly turned to mud by the constant rain. His clothing was soaked and he was hungry. Not to mention sore in a few places from the fight. Dealing with a problem was not too high up on his list after nearly being caught in a trap.

"What is it?" he asked, pushing open the door, positive Logan would be within earshot. "What's your problem?"

"My problem?" A short, squat figure turned around, freckles blazing against the ultra-pale skin. "*My* problem?"

Chief's jaw dropped. The person speaking didn't look anything like Logan. Too short. Too lush. Too *female*. But he'd recognize that shape anywhere, even without the tone and the glare.

"Sydney?" he asked, wondering what the neighbor was doing here. "What are you doing here?"

He'd met Sydney once before, the first full night they'd spent at the farmhouse, where they had celebrated one another and officially welcomed Lucien's mate Alison into their growing pack. She'd come over to complain about the noise, which apparently had been audible in her farmhouse acres away.

Chief, being the diplomat of the group, had taken her away, plied her with food and a little booze to help her relax, all in the interests of maintaining cordial relations with anyone nearby. They were trying to keep their presence at the farm a secret, after all. Couldn't have anyone blabbing and complaining about them to others. Word *would* get around.

He'd taken his relations with her a little farther than expected when they'd ended up back at her house later that night, but she hadn't minded, as long as he left after. Which he did.

Sydney's face turned practically purple in response to his question and he felt a major outburst coming. Thankfully, Logan appeared out of the nearby planning room and stepped between them, a concerned look on his face.

Glancing between the two of them, Chief's concern grew. "What did I do?" he asked, spreading his hands wide in a peace offering. Truthfully he had no idea. He hadn't seen Sydney since that night. She'd said not to call; he hadn't. It was as simple as that.

"Don't act like you don't know!" Sydney shouted, leaning around Logan's bulk, her face bright red, lips pulled back in a snarl that would make any wolf shifter proud.

If I wasn't on the receiving end of it, that is.

"But I don't know," he protested, even more confused. "I…"

She shook her head, his answer obviously not going over well. "Is that all you have to say for yourself? Really?"

Logan put up his hands to try and keep both of them calm, but it seemed to just enrage Sydney all the more. She batted his arm aside and moved around him to get closer to Chief.

"It's all I have to say when I don't even know what I did," he growled back, voice deepening as anger took hold. "If you could hold back your attitude for just a second and tell me, then maybe I could approach this in a better manner!"

Logan winced, but stayed quiet.

"Oh," Sydney laughed. "You didn't do anything wrong. If anything, you did it right. *Too* right."

Chief blinked once. Then again, slowly, turning his head to Logan.

The leader of the rebels shook his head and backed slowly away from the two of them, making his escape.

"Coward," Chief muttered under his breath, getting nothing more than what sounded an awful lot like a snicker in return. What could be so funny?

With Logan's withdrawal, they were alone, and by the sounds of it, there was nobody else in the house either. Obviously those who had been left behind knew something was coming, and had decided to vacate the area instead of being skewered by Sydney's temper. Unfortunately, Chief doubted he'd be doing the same any time soon.

The shock of seeing her was taking some time to fade. Although she'd graced his dreams several times since the party, Chief hadn't thought of her much. He hadn't been given any time to get to really know her that night, and though they'd had fun in bed, that was all it was. She wasn't the first to push him away after, and likely not the last.

Being single into his mid-forties as a shifter wasn't something Chief had planned out as a child. He'd expected to be mated and have a miniature pack of his own by now, but fate had different plans for him, it seemed. Every woman he'd been with had decided he wasn't the one. Some had visited his bed—or had him visit theirs—more than once, but that was about it. Why would he have thought Sydney any different?

She couldn't have been waiting for me to call her all this time...could she? He'd heard about women saying not to call, but secretly expecting and hoping he would, but this was taking it to a new level. He didn't want any part of that sort of crazy. No sir.

"Are you going to say anything?" she asked after a long staredown between them.

Chief shrugged lazily, pushing her buttons. She wasn't the only one who could be thoroughly frustrating and confusing. If that's what she wanted, she was going to get it.

"Nothing?"

He forced a yawn. "The way I figure it, you're the one with a bee in your bonnet. You should do the talking."

"Who even says that anymore?" she snapped.

Chief smothered the smile as she reacted just the way he'd planned. "You're upset. You still have yet to tell me why, and really, I don't go in for Twenty Questions unless I'm drinking. A lot."

"Upset? Is that what you think I am?" she asked dangerously, voice low, eyes closing to near slits.

He shrugged at her a second time, drawing the motion out, making him appear as calm and uncaring as possible. "Well, I didn't want to say that you're overreacting to the fact I never called, but fine: you're overreacting to the fact I never called. That I did exactly as you asked."

Sydney's mouth dropped open in shock, and an unsettling sensation fluttered through his stomach. This wasn't the reaction he'd expected. Fury, exasperation, more yelling. Those things he'd expected. But surprise at his choice of words? That didn't bode well. Chief was on the wrong track.

When she did finally find her voice, it was razor-sharp. "Why you idiotic, lump-headed, brain-dead, overgrown muscular *baboon!*" she shouted. "I'm not upset you didn't call!"

Chief licked his lips, thoroughly nervous and unsure of everything at this point. "So why *are* you upset then?'

Sydney began to shake. The red in her face had worked its way down to her neck as she went apoplectic. "I am not *upset!*" she hissed, spittle going everywhere. "I am furious! Beyond pissed off."

"At me?" he asked dumbly.

"No," she said with painfully false sweetness. "At the choice of wall décor in here. *Yes at you!*"

Chief nodded. "Right. But why?"

All her emotion exploded at once.

"Because, you miserable excuse for a penis, I'm pregnant!"

CHAPTER 3

"What?"

"I'm pregnant, you blue-eyed buffoon." Sydney crossed her arms and glared up at Lechiffre. It was those eyes that had done her in at the party. The way they'd looked at her, warm and compassionate. Between those, the beer and the food, it hadn't been long before she'd been in his arms, and he'd been between her legs.

After all, look at him. All muscled, veins practically jumping out from his skin when he flexed. *Or when he exerted himself other ways...* She flushed, forcing her face into a deeper glower to disguise the reaction she had to thoughts of him and her.

Sydney hadn't regretted it at the time. He had been very, well, *good* didn't begin to describe his efforts in bed. Thorough, perhaps. Unyielding. Exhausting, even. All of those were probably more accurate. But all those memories were now fogged over by the knowledge that, during their coupling, he'd not only lied to her about something important, but he'd managed to plant a baby inside her as well, thanks to said lie.

A very *unwanted* baby.

When she'd come over to his place, Sydney had repeated to herself over and over again to stay calm. To break the news to him gently *before* she took his head off for lying to her. That had failed the moment he'd waltzed inside and lazily complained, asking what was wanted of him.

How about a little respect!

"But…" Lechiffre, Chief, whatever, looked thoroughly and properly surprised.

At least he could do that properly.

"You said you were wearing protection," she snapped, voice cracking like fire as it roared ever higher. "I told you to put it on, dammit. You *lied* to me."

Lechiffre stood up immediately, his back ramrod straight. "I did *not* lie to you," he growled defensively. "I *was* wearing a condom. I put it on, and it was still on when I was done. Understood? It was still on."

Sydney considered his rebuttal. The fierceness of it, the adamant tone of his voice, but most of all she watched his eyes. They never wavered from her, except for once, down to her stomach and then back up. Normally she might be self-conscious when someone stared at her body, well aware she wasn't a physical specimen, but this time it drew a shiver.

Lechiffre wasn't staring at her stomach, he was staring past it, at the tiny child growing within her. *Their* child.

The thought made her nauseous for a moment, but her frustration at the situation spilled over, pushing it to the side as she came back to the moment. Lechiffre was speaking again.

"I would never lie about that," he said, using a finger to drive his point home.

She rolled her eyes. "Well then your ridiculous load must have leaked out the sides. Maybe you should jerk it more often so you don't have such a buildup in your pipes," she spit acidly. "Hopefully you were more polite to the other women you've slept with since!"

Sydney wasn't entirely sure why she'd said that last part. *Must be the pregnancy hormones kicking in or something.* Maybe that was why she was still tearing his head off, even if he was telling the truth about wearing a condom. Avoiding taking responsibility for her own actions. She was so busy in her own little world she barely heard Lechiffre's response.

"There hasn't been anyone since," he said quietly.

Sydney worked her jaw, not entirely sure what to say next. She was spared having to come up with anything when Lechiffre leaned in closer to her, his eyes narrowing.

"Are you sure it's *mine*?" he asked, anger barely held back as he threw her own comment back in her face by suggesting she'd slept with someone else since him.

Putting on a strong, impassive face, Sydney scoffed, waving a hand up and down her body. "Really now. *Really?* Do you think I'm just reeling guys in left, right and center? Rutting my way through town looking like this? Yes it's yours, you moron!"

She closed her mouth at the end, trying not to show how the comments affected her. They might be the truth, but she hated him all the more for making her acknowledge it openly. Sydney was no catch, and she knew it. But that wasn't the point just then. There was no categorical way it could be anyone else's *but* his. Period. Or lack of one, as she'd been experiencing.

Lechiffre muttered something that might have been "I think you look amazing", but the roaring in her ears prevented Sydney from hearing it clear enough to respond.

The fateful words she'd spoken to Lechiffre were rising up in her again.

I'm pregnant.

It was the first time she'd said the words out loud to anyone. Until then, it had all seemed like it could be some sort of bad dream. A nightmare that she would eventually awaken from, perhaps. Anything but reality. Now another person knew her secret, and that made it real. There was no more denying it, as she'd been doing for nearly two weeks since her period failed to arrive.

Now she had to face the consequences of their actions that night. She. Not Lechiffre. He didn't have to do anything. He had the easy part. Stick his dick in, move it around, and then voila. Deed done. Now she would suffer. Even if it was partly her own fault.

Looking at the big man, she noted the glaze to his eyes. He might be facing her, but his eyes were anywhere *but* on her. It was a stark contrast to the last time she'd seen him, when his eyes had blazed with a fervent sapphire light as they drank in every inch of her in a way no man had done before.

Even just now, staring at his big, broad shoulders as they strained at the seams of his slate gray t-shirt, or the point of his diamond-shaped face, powerful jaw tight with the news she'd just broken to him, all of that came together to remind her of the way he'd treated her that one night.

It had been more than good. But not enough to warrant what she was now going to go through. No pleasure was worth that. Not to her.

Sensing that Lechiffre was useless, and needing some space, Sydney turned and headed outside, onto the big wraparound porch that the house sported. Almost immediately her skin tightened as the cooler evening air washed over it, and the wet, heavy air dampened her almost imperceptibly.

Rain continued to splatter down, the big drops making a pleasant low rumble on the roof. It was a sound she'd fallen asleep too many times over the past few years since she'd bought the little hobby farm next door. It was peaceful, reminding her of a different time, one of the few pleasant memories of her youth.

Pregnant. With child. Knocked up. A filled womb.

A tremor ran through her body until she gripped the railing tight, clenching her muscles so they stopped. It was a foreign idea to her, one that she'd rarely thought about now that she was into her thirties.

Should have had the damn surgery to prevent this, woman. Now you're going to pay.

She would pay, yes. But not the child. They would have a better life, one with a mother fit to raise them. Sydney thought about it, but the truth was, she knew she didn't have the strength within her to see everything through to completion. She was too weak. Too unprepared.

CHAPTER 4

Pregnant. Pregnant. Pregnant.

The word bounced around his brain like an echo chamber. Fading, fading, then bouncing back stronger again, on repeat. There was little he could do about it, his brain refused to cooperate. It was still frozen, locked in paralysis after hearing her say the words.

But I was so careful.

Shifter DNA was potent, especially when mixed with a human. Usually if the female was on birth control, there were no issues. Those drugs seemed to work. Not this time. Either that or Sydney wasn't on any.

The more he thought about it, the more Chief became confident that was the case. Considering the way she'd dismissed his claim about her sleeping with other people, and how adamant she'd been the day they hooked up that he put on a condom, it seemed to indicate she wasn't using any protection herself, because she didn't expect to need it.

It was a shame that more men didn't see her attractiveness for what it was, but now wasn't the time for Chief to dwell upon that. Despite his efforts, some of his sperm had clearly escaped and impregnated her.

Accidents like this weren't exactly uncommon among the shifter population, but they weren't frequent either. Most males did their best to prevent it from happening. They were meant to procreate with their mates. Not the multitude of human women who would gladly throw themselves at shifters simply because of their looks.

That was all well and fun for a younger shifter. One going through puberty or just learning their place in the world. For a seasoned veteran like Chief, who was into his forties now, he rarely took advantage of the blessings of his heritage. To him, sex should have a stronger meaning, a more intimate connection, between the two parties.

He was fairly positive it was the way Sydney had stormed into the middle of their party and told everyone to shut up that had attracted him that night. As the diplomat of the pack, he'd found himself taking her aside to try and calm her down. By the end of the night they'd found comfort in each other's arms.

She hadn't wanted him to stay, probably because she was embarrassed at having slept with him so quickly, and Chief had respected her wishes, leaving and not calling. Now he wished he'd thought things through more thoroughly. It was his responsibility to prevent things like this from happening.

I'm going to be a father. Sydney is going to be a mother.

That, more than anything, was likely what was freaking her out. He didn't blame her for the way she was reacting. Dealing with such unexpected news on her own would have left anyone worked up. Once they had a chance to calm down and talk it over, he was positive she would see all the wonderful things that were to come.

She might not be his mate, but Chief had always wanted to be a father. A *father*. Even just thinking the word brought a wide, cheek-splitting grin to his face. Something he'd dreamt about since he was young was finally going to bless his life. A child. Would it be a little boy, maybe? Or a little human princess he could spoil?

"Well you've certainly got a shit-eating-grin on your face. What's the occasion?" It was Logan, he was back. The leader of the rebels sauntered back into the room.

"Nothing," Chief said quickly. Too quickly.

Logan quirked an eyebrow at him. "Really. Does it have anything to do with the human on the porch looking utterly lost and forlorn?"

"Forlorn?" Chief asked, straightening.

"Downright devastated, if you ask me," Logan told him, without an ounce of sarcasm. "What did you do to her?"

Chief bit his lip, debating for a moment on whether to tell him. "She is with child."

Logan started to nod, freezing halfway through the motion. "You mean *your* child, don't you?"

"Who the hell else do you think I mean?" Chief snapped, running his hands through his hair, the unruly black strands momentarily straightening before resuming their loose, almost wavy curls.

"Why are you in here then?" Logan wanted to know. "Shouldn't you two be like, celebrating or something?"

Chief headed for the door. "I guess maybe we're not in a celebrating mood."

Logan was right about one thing. Chief shouldn't be inside. He should be out there, with Sydney, helping her come to terms with this new development. Letting her know that he would be there the entire way, physically and financially, for her. Most of his money was locked down by the Houses accounts, but he had enough hidden away, as did any shifter worth his name. Maybe knowing that would help put her at ease.

"Sydney," he said, pausing several feet away as he found her just like Logan had said, on the edge of the porch, leaning against the railing as she stared up at the night sky, the last of the clouds finally drifting away to reveal the twinkling beauty of billions of stars hovering above them, seemingly *just* out of reach.

She turned slightly at her name, acknowledging him, but not taking her eyes off the sky.

"We should talk about this," he said, trying to hold in his excitement. "I know you're nervous, but it's going to be okay. We can do this. We can raise this child together. Whether it's a boy or a girl, they'll be well looked after. They can play sports, or dance, or whatever they want to do. And when they get old enough they—"

Chief cut himself off when it became apparent Sydney wasn't paying attention to him. She wasn't ignoring him, but her attention was elsewhere. Upward. He frowned, glancing at her from head to toe a second time.

Her fingers were wrapped around the railing so tight the knuckles were turning white. The space between her shoulder blades was thick with knots and tension, pulling her chest back even while she stared up at the sky, her face a mask, hiding her emotion. How could he not have seen this? Her entire body language was screaming something at him that he'd shoved to the side in his own joy.

Sydney wasn't excited about this. At all. It was anathema to him. As a shifter, he valued offspring as high, or higher, than just about anything besides his mate. If he had one. They were life's most precious gift, to be treasured and cherished. But that wasn't Sydney's outlook. Something had soured her on it, and now she wasn't happy.

Hauling back his boundless enthusiasm, Chief took the two strides forward until he was standing next to her, leaning on the railing as well. His eyes tracked through the sky, picking out patterns and constellations with trained experience.

"It sure is a shame the city dwellers can't experience a sky like this," he muttered softly.

"It's our little secret," she replied distantly. "I'm not too keen on sharing."

Chuckling to himself he nodded, knowing full well how she felt. "That's my favorite constellation," he told her, pointing off to the left, across her body.

"Which one is that? Lots of stars over there." Sydney followed his finger, but there was no way for her to tell which constellation he was referring to.

"Lupus," he said, finger tracing the line in the stars.

"The wolf," she said, identifying it.

"Mmmm. It won't be fully visible until June of course, but I know where it is."

Sydney nodded, then pointed up higher into the night sky. "I like the Big Dipper, personally, as cliché as that is."

Chief tried to suppress a scowl, but he knew he failed when Sydney asked him what the problem was.

"The Big Dipper is part of Ursa Major," he explained. "That's my least favorite constellation."

"Riiighht," Sydney said, then surprised both of them with a laugh at the perceived silliness of his comment. She immediately looked away.

"I want you to know something," he said tersely, deciding now was as good a time as any to say what he had to say.

"What's that?" She didn't look back, her neck muscles tensing as she waited for him to speak.

"I'm going to be there. For you and the child. Throughout the entire thing. Even if you and I aren't... aren't a thing. I'm going to be there to support you. Physically. Monetarily. Whatever it takes. I'm not going anywhere this time."

Something wet splashed against his hand as he gripped the railing, and for a moment Chief thought the rain had returned, something falling from a clear sky. But it wasn't rain. It was a tear, having fallen from Sydney's cheek. He stiffened as she cried silently next to him. What had he done wrong? What should he do now?

Paralyzed by confusion at the situation, Chief simply did nothing at all. He stood there and let her cry, fighting the urge to wrap his arm around her and pull Sydney close to him. They weren't together, not like that. He needed to respect her desire for distance. The last time they'd touched, she'd wound up pregnant. He didn't want to make things worse.

"No thank you."

Facing her fully now, Chief leaned in a little closer. "Pardon?"

"I...I appreciate your offer, Lechiffre, but no. I don't think so. I...I can't do this." The tears flowed faster now, practically obscuring her eyes from him, the deep brown already almost invisible in the dark of light.

"What do you mean?" he asked, a horrible sensation flowing out from his stomach as fear spread its tendrils deep into him. "Are you...are you..." He couldn't even bring himself to think of it.

"I can't do this, Chief. The child needs a family, a mother...a family that can give it what it deserves. That's not me. I'm going to give it up for adoption," she stated, her eyes locking onto his, daring him to argue with her.

CHAPTER 5

Bracing herself, Sydney prepared to defend her decision to him. Her points were lined up and in order.

"What?" Lechiffre just sort of stared at her, uncomprehending.

"I can't be the sort of mother a child brought into this world deserves," she said, falling back onto her strongest point. "The child, it needs to be loved, to be spoiled, to be well taken care of. To have a family who can give it all those things. Not a washed up farmer who can't even keep a houseplant alive. Once it's born, I'll be giving it up for adoption. It's the *right* move." She crossed her arms and dared him to challenge her.

Sydney's decision was set in stone. All her adult life, she had told herself she didn't want children. Told her friends she wasn't interested in being a mother. Now that she was pregnant, she was more terrified than ever about the concept, and didn't see any other decision available to her. Not one she could live with, at least.

"You can't be serious."

Pushing off the railing she paced back and forth along the front of the railing, biting her lip, fingers twitching nervously until she shoved them into her pockets to try and ignore the distraction.

"I'm completely serious," she said. "That's the decision I've come to. It's the best one for the child."

"I'll take them."

She scoffed loudly. "Right. You just moved onto this farm from goodness knows where. You live here with twenty other workout freaks. You party regularly, and fight often as well."

Lechiffre quirked an eyebrow.

"I live next door. I hear the moans of pain sometimes when you come back. Noise carries in the dark. I also know you have some big-ass dogs around here some-where, though I've never seen them. I've heard 'em, though."

The big man stiffened at that, his eyes narrowing, and for a moment Sydney thought he was going to lose his composure. Had she hit a nerve of some sort? That wasn't her goal in all this.

"What I'm saying," she continued, "is that this is abso-lutely *not* the sort of place to raise a child, and you are simply not the right person to raise one amidst all this either. The child will be better off in a home with those who will care for and love them. Not with either of us. Come on Lechiffre, you know that. This is no place for a baby." She waved around them.

A moment later there was the sound of shouting and a meaty *thwack* as flesh connected with flesh. Someone yelped in pain, there were a few more shouts, and just like that, the peaceful night dissolved into discord.

"Another fight," she muttered. "Why am I not surprised?"

Lechiffre looked ready to lose his temper, but she was right, and what's more, Sydney *knew* she had the right of it. There was no solid argument he could make to counter that. Not after such a perfect example of the reasons why he wouldn't make a good parent were thrown right in front of them.

"It's my child too," he growled quietly. "I can be a parent."

"Chief," she said, using the informal version of his name that she knew he preferred over the clunky long-form. "Come on now. Whatever is going on in your life. Whatever all you *men* are doing out here living together, fighting together…doing everything together, it's not a place fit for a child. This isn't a family environment. You can't provide that. Neither can I. *We* certainly can't," she finished with a laugh. "This is the right choice. You know it is, deep down. So please, don't fight me on it."

He fell silent, and this time it was his turn to stare blankly up into the night sky. Sydney watched the muscles in his back tense and relax several times over. His arms strained against the sleeves of his shirt. He was angry.

Was he mad at her for making the decision, or mad at himself because she was right? It was hard to tell, really.

"Why are you so confident that I couldn't do this?" he asked.

"Chief," she protested, sagging. "It's not like that! It's

not that I think you couldn't do this. It's that I don't think you're in a place to do it *right now*. Neither am I. I wish this wasn't the situation, believe me, I do. I had my life happy and perfect the way it was."

And lonely.

"Then I met you," she continued, ignoring herself. "I let myself have a moment of unguarded fun, when I knew I shouldn't have. Now I'm pregnant, and that means I have to make the tough choices, the *smart* choices." She felt an almost irrational calm descend over her like a wet blanket as she spoke, the words coming from deep within her.

The anger she'd felt earlier was mostly gone. When Chief had told her that he hadn't lied, that he *had* been using protection, the basis for most of her anger went out the window. Like a good fire it had taken time for her fury to turn to embers and eventually burn out. Once the heat was gone, all that was left was the cold, hard fear. And the truth.

"I wish it hadn't happened," she said, forcing herself to ignore the hurt on his face. She'd meant the pregnancy, not hooking up with him, and she could tell he thought she meant him, but it didn't matter just then. "But it's the truth. I thought about running away, but that won't get me anywhere. I'm sort of stuck carrying this thing wherever I go," she said with a wry laugh. "Can't really outrun it."

Yes, the anger was gone now. It had given way to a sadness. One that she'd been trying to understand before Chief had come outside. There were parts to it that didn't make sense. She felt sadness for the loss of her life the way she knew it. Of the changes that would overcome her body, among other things. But there was something more. Something else she hadn't quite identified.

Perhaps it was related to her. Or her and kids. Whatever it was, she couldn't let it affect her decision, not now. She couldn't afford to play the what-if game.

What *if* she'd never become pregnant in the first place?

What *if* things had happened differently between her and Lechiffre?

What *if* she kept the child?

What *if* she could be a good mother?

That last one was the most laughable of the lot. If anyone knew anything about her, they would be well aware she wasn't fit to be a mother, good *or* bad. Sydney wasn't mother material of any kind, even if she didn't have a thing against kids themselves.

"What can I do, then?" Chief asked solemnly, interrupting her internal stream of thoughts.

"Honestly?" she asked, half to him, half to the open air around them. "Right now, I think I need some space. To leave me be. I...I had to come tell you. You deserved that." She winced. "I also had to find out if this was your fault or not. But right now, I just can't be around you. I need to deal with this, and I can't with you."

She needed to be away from Chief and his stupidly handsome face, big, delicious muscles, and the constant reminder of what those big hands of his felt like on her hips, legs, breasts... She was getting flushed even thinking about it.

"I need to go," she said tautly, turning and fleeing into the night, leaving him standing there on the porch, most likely staring after her.

Sydney didn't look back. She couldn't. If she did, the strength that had somehow prevented her from letting those fabulous arms embrace her might fail, and she couldn't have that.

Not again.

CHAPTER 6

Chief was struggling.

The leadership cabal was meeting in the planning room. It consisted of Logan, their leader; Lucien, the second in command; himself; and Linden, the head guard and man in charge of security of the property.

His mind kept wandering as Logan talked, pointing occasionally at maps and stressing points. They were talking about... He frowned. What *was* it they were talking about again?

Sydney. That was what was dominating his mind. She was there, constantly, every time he closed his eyes.

I'm giving the child up for adoption.

Two days later, and he was still having trouble reconciling the fact that it had come out of her mouth. She didn't want the child. *His* child.

She was right, though. On one level at least. The farmhouse wasn't a place to raise a baby. Sydney was wrong about the reason, however. The people he lived with, they were all shifters. Every shifter, male or female, was born with an instinctual love for children. Adding new pups to the pack was one of the greatest joys a male could experience, after finding one's mate.

Chief didn't blame Sydney for not understanding that, of course. How could he? Their secret was one they guarded ferociously. He made a mental note to mention to Linden that the men needed to shut up in wolf form. They were making too much noise. If Sydney could hear them at her place, then others could too.

It wouldn't take long for word to get around and reach the Tyrant-King back at Moonshadow Manor that a bunch of giant dogs were living on a farm on the outskirts of town. He would see through that in a heartbeat, sending his men to destroy the rebellion before they could truly get organized.

That was why the farm wasn't a place for an infant. With the threat of fighting, and quite possibly even death hovering over his head, Chief knew he couldn't bring Sydney or his unborn child to live with him on the farm. Not when he couldn't guarantee their safety. They would be better off on her farm until the internal schism tearing House Canis apart was settled.

"What do you think, Chief?'

He looked up as someone said his name. The trio were all looking at him expectantly.

"Uhhh."

"Did you hear a word we just said?" Lucien asked.

"Sorry." Chief shrugged apologetically. "Run it by me one more time?"

"You need to focus," Logan said with a slight sharpness

to his voice. He knew what was on Chief's mind, but that bite to his voice informed Chief that this was serious enough that he needed him to put his personal situation aside for the moment and focus.

Chief nodded. He would try. Sydney would want him to do that. To keep up what he was doing. It would set a good example for their child and— *Focus!*

"We've been talking about our numbers," Logan repeated. "We need to rally more to our side."

This tired argument again. "What exactly do you want us to do?" Chief asked. "We've liaised with every splinter group we know about, and even two we didn't. We went from eight to twenty-three in the span of six weeks. That's pretty good growth, not to mention we have no idea how many others who have fled the Manor are still out there."

The others muttered angrily among themselves. Although the rebels had worked furiously to track down anyone and everyone who had fled, trying to persuade them to join up, the Tyrant-King Laurien and his followers had been doing the same.

Except when they found anyone, they rounded them up and dragged them back to the Manor. Forcefully. After five weeks, the rebels hadn't been able to find any other stragglers nearby. So they'd started talking about other plans; ways to increase their numbers.

"There are many back at the Manor who support us," Logan countered. "They just have no way of getting out."

Chief snorted. They'd been down this path before. "That's because that bastard sitting on the Throne has over a hundred men patrolling the house and the walls ensuring none of them leave. Sure, there's probably forty or fifty more that would outright support us, and another hundred or so who simply don't know what to do. But we don't have the strength to go in there. Look what happened last night. We nearly lost a third of our strength to a mere ten of them, simply because we were so desperate to gain more supporters. Imagine if they'd sent twenty men after us. We'd have been screwed."

The others looked away, upset and frustrated, because he was right. Anyone who wasn't supporting either side had made themselves scarce, leaving the Manor and Plymouth Falls for the safety of larger cities, farther away. There simply were no more refugees to gather up. That phase of the fighting was done with. The two sides had gathered their strength, and the rebels had been found wanting.

Chief's mind turned toward Sydney as the others began to bicker over their own individual plans on how they should best try to even the odds. He'd heard it all before, and it always ended up the same. None of them would work the way they wanted. There were flaws in every plan.

Now I need to find the flaws in her plan to give up the child to an adoption agency.

There was no way he could let that happen. Especially if the child was a male. Growing up in a human family, when the shifter blood began to course through his veins at the onset of puberty, things would get *very* awkward. Everyone knows different types of hair starts to grow at that point, but the textbooks don't say anything about an entire coat of fur suddenly springing out of your skin without warning.

But he needed to find a way to do this *with* Sydney's support. That was important to him, for reasons he couldn't yet figure out. Simply taking the child from the adoption agency wasn't an option. The brute force approach wasn't open to him, not this time. Chief would need to use his diplomatic skills to their utmost if he was going to convince her to change her mind.

But he would. Somehow. This was *his* child as much as hers. He would have a say. Hopefully.

"I have an idea."

Everyone turned to Linden.

"We're not going to the bears," Lucien snapped. "For the last time, give it up already. We will solve this on our own, one way or another, understood?"

Linden growled at the tone, knuckles popping as he squeezed them tightly. The quartet all stood around a circular table, upon which were spread maps of Plymouth Falls and the surrounding areas, as well as far more detailed maps of their local setting, marked with patrol routes and other bits of information necessary to those who oversaw the entire farm.

"Yes, I know. You're all too stubborn and egotistical to go that route," Linden said calmly. "I understand that, even if I disagree with it. They hate the Tyrant-King Laurien as much as we do, *but*, your pride won't let you ask for help from non-Canis. Fine. Then we should ask for help from our own kind."

Logan stood up straight, regarding his de facto captain thoughtfully, eyes squinting slightly. "Who do you have in mind?" he said at last.

"Why don't we ask the Pacific pack?" Linden suggested.

The room was silent for a moment. Then it exploded as Logan and Lucien both spoke at once.

"Absolutely not!" Logan bellowed.

"Are you crazy?" Lucien snapped. "There is no way that's a good idea."

Linden, however, didn't back down easily. Chief watched him, keeping his opinions to himself, interested to see how the guard leader would defend his choice.

"It's a solid idea," Linden countered. "They despise Laurien. That's *why* they disavowed our house and moved to the west coast, into the mountains."

"Right, and they have closed their borders to anyone, and want nothing to do with our House or the shifter world. They are outcasts, and that's the way they want it," Logan said, slamming a fist onto the table. "Come on, we need better ideas than that nonsense!"

Chief leaned forward, his brain spinning a mile a minute. The Pacific pack were a large group of wolf shifters who eschewed any larger loyalty or affiliation with House Canis, the shifter courts or the politics that governed the paranormal world as a whole. They simply wanted nothing to do with it, and they would do anything to ensure it stayed that way.

They also, according to the last report he'd heard, were nearing a hundred members in strength. If they supported the rebels against the Tyrant-King, then many others would likely voice their support. Some of the small big-city packs might even leave the confines of their towers and city parks to return home. That last seemed unlikely, but one never knew.

It could change the war though, that was for certain. In fact, there were multiple uses he could think of.

"I think we should do it," he said.

Logan and Lucien both turned to stare at him, mouths open in shock. "You can't be serious?" Logan challenged.

"Deadly. Linden is right. We are out of options here. We need to think big, and think bold if we're going to have a hope in hell of overthrowing that asshole and putting your ass on the throne. We need them. We need Lenard's support on this one, and you know it, Logan."

Lenard was the Alpha of the Pacific pack. Their leader, and the one who, ten years earlier, had led the first of his pack in their split with the House.

"You agree with him?" Lucien was shocked.

"Yes, I do. We need the help. Get over it. This isn't about *us*. It's about our House. We need to be willing to do whatever it takes to make us whole again. That means *everyone*." Chief crossed his arms, staring the two leaders down, daring them to come up with a counterargument.

"Shit," Logan muttered after a moment. "He's right."

"Of course I'm right. Linden's idea is a good one."

"Thank you," Linden said, tilting his head sharply. "I appreciate the support."

They waited for the other two to come to grips with the decision, but it didn't take long. That was one reason why Chief supported Logan as the rightful King of House Canis. He was open to suggestions and even changing his mind if he was presented with a proper and compelling argument. The man could accept constructive criticism.

The Tyrant-King would have thrown him in a cell by now, or worse. It was a stark difference in ruling technique, and one Chief was glad to throw his support behind.

Especially because it would be a great way to get Sydney away from the fighting and give him a chance to convince her to keep their child. Or at least let him raise it. Yes, this was the best choice available to them.

"I'll go," he said, answering the next, unspoken question. "I'm the best choice."

"I'll go with you," Logan offered, but Chief shook his head. "No, we need everyone else here. I'll go. Alone."

Mostly.

CHAPTER 7

"Dammit!" she swore, sucking on her thumb, the hammer falling to the ground. "Stupid."

Leaning against the fence post, Sydney cursed the damn cattle and their nosy ways. How was it they always seemed to find a way out, without fail, every few months? It wasn't fair. Couldn't her fence stay together just *one* season without needing a dozen repairs?

"Screw you, Ethel," she muttered to the big brown and white heifer nearby.

The cow lowed at her softly, as if the animal could understand.

"I'm sorry," she apologized, feeling guilty even if the cow didn't know what she was saying. "It's not your fault. It's not you I'm mad at, and I shouldn't be taking it out on you."

Truthfully, Sydney wasn't quite sure why she was mad. Perhaps pregnancy hormones were messing with her already. For the past three days she'd been moodier than hell, and it was driving her up the wall.

"Stupid Lechiffre. Had to go and get me knocked up. It's all his fault, really."

Deep down, Sydney knew it was as much her fault as his, but taking her anger out on him since he wasn't there felt better than berating herself.

To his credit, he'd left her alone. Again. Just like she'd asked him to. The first time she had been perfectly content with that. A night of fun, a morning hangover, and then she was back to her life, the way she liked it. Always busy, no time to slow down and think about anything else.

Now Chief was leaving her alone, and for some reason she was angry at him for it. Muttering to herself about needing to make up her mind, Sydney picked up the hammer and started driving the nail into the wood crossbeam of the fence, paying more attention to the direction of her swing this time.

With each swing she took out some of her anger, trying to let it dissipate. It was her own fault that Chief wasn't there. Nothing she could do about that, unless she was willing to back down and ask him to come see her. Which she wouldn't do.

That would be tantamount to inviting him into her life, and accepting that he would be around throughout the entire pregnancy. Which she couldn't have. Especially if she was going to keep her hands off him and his scorching hot bod.

"Why couldn't you have been ugly?" she growled.

"So we're agreed. You *are* beautiful."

Sydney was in mid-backswing when the voice sounded

from behind her, and she let go of the shaft by accident, yelping in surprise at the unexpected voice.

"Is that how you treat all your guests?" the voice asked humorously.

Turning slowly, Sydney winced at the sight of Chief standing several strides behind her, holding the hammer about a foot away from his crotch. She was kneeling to fix the fence, and with his height...

"Well this is incredibly awkward," she mumbled, finally tearing her eyes away from his crotch and the poignant reminder of how good it had felt inside her. "Sorry about that."

He nodded and flipped the hammer around, extending it to her butt-first. She took it and slipped it into a loop hanging from her jeans.

"What are you doing here?" Sydney almost kept her tone neutral. Almost. "Are you spying on me?"

Chief frowned. "What?"

"Never mind," she said, waving it off. "What can I do for you?"

So formal and uptight. Sydney wished she could relax around him, but the last time she'd done that, he'd put a child inside of her. She wasn't about to go back down that route again. No sir.

"Well, I know you said you wanted to be alone," he began. "But I wanted to check in on you, see how you were doing now that we've both had a bit of time to process this. I promise I won't make this a regular thing without your permission, but I felt like just this once, at least, I probably should."

BLOOD MATE

Sydney was touched by his thoughtfulness, if nothing else. But that didn't change a thing.

"I'm still set on adoption, if that's what you're really asking about," she said, crossing her arms, prepared to stand her ground. "It's not really up for negotiation."

Something appeared and then disappeared in Chief's eyes as he got himself under control. It was gone too fast for her to process *what*, but Sydney had seen it. He was bothered by her decision. A lot.

Would he be able to accept the decision? Maybe, she decided, she should make some effort to bring him around to understanding why this was the best choice not only for them both, but also for the child itself. If he could be brought to see, then it would make the next nine months a lot easier on both of them.

"This is my child as well, Sydney. I feel like I should have some say in what happens after it's born."

That was a fair point, but not one that, ultimately in the long run, mattered. Not to her. She couldn't have the child stay nearby. A constant reminder of him, and of…of other things. No, it had to go with some anonymous family far, far away. One that would provide it a life not on the farm. A proper childhood. A mother. Things she simply could not provide for it. Didn't he understand? This was about *her* failure.

"I'm sorry, Lechiffre, but no. Adoption is the way to go. Trust me, you'll understand in time." Returning her attention to the fencepost, Sydney waited for him to get the hint and leave.

"Why are you so scared about the possibility of keeping

47

this child?" he asked, fingers closing around the hammer as she raised it.

Sydney growled and pulled, trying to get him to release his grip, but the hammer didn't budge. How strong *was* he?

"I'm not scared," she snapped, yanking at the hammer.

Chief's arm might have swayed an inch. She'd used all her strength to try and move him. Were his muscles made from steel or something? She eyed the bulge of his arm, but it didn't even seem like he was trying particularly hard.

A memory of him easily tossing her around the bedroom rushed back, a prominent reminder that even her round frame hadn't been a challenge for him to manhandle when he wanted to switch things up. It had certainly been fun, that was for sure, especially when he'd—

Enough.

Chief was looking at her now, his face relaxed, eyebrows slightly raised, mouth pulled a little to one side in the universal expression of "I don't believe a word you're saying."

Well, too bad. She didn't owe him any answers about anything. He wasn't her husband. Just some random she'd let into her bedroom for a night of heated passion and rough sex.

Even just thinking about the things he'd done to her had Sydney's breasts tingling in her bra, nipples hardening into nubs at the fresh reminder of the warmth of his mouth and tongue around them. Or between her legs, where a fire was ignited anew.

Stop it. No more. You don't need him for pleasure. Sure, he's definitely better than doing it solo, but he's not necessary. Not his thick, strong fingers that found all your sensual spots, nor the firmness of his tongue as he planted himself between your legs and refused to stop until—

"I'm not scared," she repeated, adding what she hoped was a firm nod to the end.

"Right. Okay, well, I think you need to do something to relax."

She was about to protest, but this time Chief kept on talking, not letting her get a word in.

"So, we're going to go on a trip. You and I. And baby."

Sydney blinked. "Run that by me one more time. It sounded like you said we're going on a trip. Together."

Of all the terrible ideas…

"That's exactly what said."

She nodded. Slowly. Exaggerating the motion. "Try again."

"You and me. Together. Leave this place for a bit. Go somewhere else. Vay-cay-shun."

By the time he finished speaking in his drawn-out, simplistic manner, she was glaring at him. "Thank you for treating me like I'm ten. I understand the concept. What I don't get is why you think I'm going somewhere? I have a farm to manage, in case you haven't paid any attention to anything, except what you want."

"It'll be fine. I'm sure your lead hand could take care of it while we're gone."

"Let's assume you're right," she said, crossing her arms, hammer sticking out from her left side. "I'm still waiting to find out why I should go on vacation with you. Or why I *would*?"

"You really need to stop putting the blame solely on me

for this situation," Chief said, his voice tightening ever so slightly.

"I'm not," she denied hotly.

They both knew she was lying.

"I looked it up," he said. "Lots of people do it nowadays. They call it a babymoon." He chuckled. "Ridiculous name, but I like the idea. So we should do it."

"*Couples* do that, Chief. Married people do that. Strangers who accidentally get pregnant, they don't do that."

"So we'll start a new trend," he pronounced, standing upright, his shirt pulling taut across his massive chest, distracting her.

"I don't think that would be a good idea. Thank you for the thoughtfulness, but no. I have work to do around here."

She waited for Chief to leave. He didn't. Instead, he kept staring at her, tapping his chin.

"What?" she finally asked, exasperated.

"Well you see, that could be a problem." There was a twinkle in his eyes. He was enjoying this!

"What could be a problem?" she asked when he didn't continue. She hated leading sentences like that. Just spit it all out at once; don't make her ask a useless question.

"You not coming."

Grrr.

"*Why* is me not coming a problem?" Her hand tightened over the handle of the hammer. For a brief instant she imagined smacking it against him, but knowing her luck it would probably just bounce off his chest and fly back into her face. Those muscles were harder than steel.

"For one, the trip is already booked," Chief said.

"*What?!*" she yelped. "Why would you do something like that?"

"It was a deal too good to pass up?" He shrugged apologetically.

Sydney couldn't quite believe what she was hearing. Of all the insane, idiotic things he could have done, booking a trip for the two of them to go somewhere had to be up near the top. She didn't even *know* him! What made him think she was going to hop on a plane and go spend a week or whatever somewhere with him?

"I can't begin to tell you how much is wrong with this," she groaned. "You can't just do this to people Chief. That's called guilting them into something. How am I supposed to say no, now that you've gone and spent money on this?" She tugged at her hair, the short pixie cut immediately flopping back into place.

You forgot your hat.

The stray thought elicited a smile on her face at its sheer randomness.

"You're smiling," Chief said, perking up. "Does that mean you're considering it?"

She shook her head. "I don't think so, Chief, I'm sorry. It's just not a good idea." She paused. "You'll just have to find some other woman to drag down south with."

"South?" he tilted his head.

"Yeah. South. You know, beaches and sand. That's usually where people go for babymoons. To relax, because it's the last time they'll be able to for a while after a child is born." He was staring at her, nodding slowly. "Where did you book it for?" she asked, curiosity getting the better of her.

"Cross country trip," he said, beaming. "To the mountains. Maybe the coast after."

"Ah." Sydney licked her lips, trying to think of a way to let him down gently.

"So you're going to come though, right?"

"I don't know, Chief," she half-moaned, frustrated at the position he'd put her in. Backing her into a corner like this wasn't overly nice. And yet, he was *trying* to do right by her, even if he was screwing up while doing so. There was some niceness in the gesture. Wasn't there?

"Come on. You said you were thinking of running away. This is our chance!"

She gaped at him. "How did you remember that?" And more importantly, how did he translate *her* running away into *them* taking a trip together to celebrate a child she wasn't fit to bring into the world? It was so ass-backwards she couldn't even begin to understand how he'd made the connection.

"I listen to what you have to say?"

Sydney's lips parted in a silent moan of protest. How was she supposed to say no *now*?

Would it really be that bad a thing to go somewhere? It's not like I don't have a lot to learn and prepare for. And I'm not going to be able to run the farm throughout the entire pregnancy. Jose or Andy are going to have to step up eventually. This could be a good trial run and oh god am I actually thinking of going?

She was. She actually was. The idea of going somewhere *was* appealing. Sydney had never left Plymouth Falls except for a trip to an all-inclusive on her twenty-first birthday, the first and only time she'd done something like that.

"So you're going to come, right?" Chief asked, smiling at her, face filled with hope.

"I…"

"Please?"

Did he just bounce up and down with excitement?

She sighed, hands fidgeting nervously. "I guess?"

There, she'd committed to going. It was done, nothing more that she could say about it now.

"Yes!" Chief pumped his fist in celebration. "This is going to a good time, I promise."

She shrugged, envisioning roaring fires in a mountain-side chalet while she relaxed under a huge blanket, only revealing her hands to take the cup of hot chocolate he would bring to her. Things *could* be worse.

"Okay. Okay," she said with a laugh as he continued to bounce around excitedly. "I'll put it in the calendar and talk to my lead hands about running it while we're gone. When did you book it for?"

Chief stood up straight, puffing out that magnificent chest of his. "Pack your things Sydney, we leave tomorrow!"

"What?!"

CHAPTER 8

"Chief, I have to admit, this isn't quite the trip I envisioned when you said cross country to the mountains."

"It's not?"

She shook her head, looking over at him from the passenger seat, curled up under a warm blanket. *That* much at least had come true.

"I kind of figured we would fly across the country, where a car would whisk us away into the mountains to stay at a beautiful log chalet with a gorgeous lookout across the valley. Big fires, gorgeous landscapes, and lots of relaxation." She looked out the rear view mirror as they pulled onto the highway from the latest gas station to stop at.

"The last thing I expected was roadside motels and cold breakfasts driving across the country." To be fair to him, though, the motel they'd left this morning had had a waffle bar, which was an unexpected treat.

Chief chewed on his lower lip. "I'm sorry," he said at last. "I should have given you the details."

"Maybe," she agreed, not feeling overly upset. It was still nice to get out of Plymouth Falls. "But I should have asked as well. I just sort of assumed."

They'd left the day before, which was when she'd first realized her erroneous assumption about the type of trip they were taking. When Chief had said cross-country, she'd assumed they were simply travelling *across the country*. Not that he wanted to drive across it, instead of fly.

She'd kept her mouth shut for the first day of driving, not wanting to come off as rude and whiny right away. Even now, she felt bad bringing it up, but if there were any more surprises coming her way, Sydney wanted to know about them *now*, instead of later. Like, what was their final destination?

These were the sorts of questions she should have asked at the start, but she'd let her preconceptions get the better of her, and she'd trusted Chief. That, perhaps, was where things had gone wrong. Going all the way back to the day she'd come over to their party to ask them to turn it down a notch, and ended up letting him into her bed.

"I promise, I'll make it up to you," Chief said, startling her by breaking the silence. "I just thought this would be fun for us. Get to spend some time together, learn a bit more about one another."

Sydney was studying him while he spoke, trying to discern if his eagerness was false or not. Everything she could pick up made it seem like he was being honest and forthcoming. Genuine. Did he actually want to know more about her? Why?

"It's not the *worst* trip I've ever been on," she lied, not wanting him to realize how poorly-travelled and experienced she was. "In fact it's not really a bad trip at all. You've been perfectly polite, made sure the rooms had two bedrooms, stopping regularly for, um, pit stops."

"You're not completely miserable?" he asked, perking up slightly.

"Absolutely not," she said with a laugh. "I said it's not what I expected. Not that it's been terrible. If nothing else, I'm learning a lot about the places we pass."

Chief practically beamed at her comment. As soon as he'd learned that she hadn't travelled this route before, he'd become a walking, talking encyclopedia of information. *That* place there was where some famous so-and-so had opened his first store. Just down that road and around the corner, supposedly, was a famous battle site for some war she'd barely even heard about hundreds of years ago. That fake tree was the sixth tallest fake tree in the country. And so on, and so on, until her ears bled.

But, despite it all, she hadn't found it within her to stop. After all, he was doing it to show her the country they lived in, because he thought it was helping. She didn't have the heart to tell him that random trivia just wasn't something that interested her. But it made him happy, and didn't cost her anything, so she kept silent when he started to ramble.

"I'm glad to hear it," he said, putting both hands on the wheel as they went around a particularly sharp bend in the two-lane highway, the ground sloped sharply up on the right.

They were getting closer to the mountains now, and the ground was beginning to reflect that. The plains were behind them, and the ground was jagged and filled with hills that rose and fell abruptly, creating an uneven landscape that could change in a heartbeat. A moment later, the road straightened and broke into a meadow between hills, before diving back between two peaks just ever so short to be termed mountains.

Signs warned of the potential for falling rocks, and the steepness of the man-made cut they drove through blocked much of the remaining sunlight, only a few rays filtering in. After another thirty seconds, even that was gone, only the ambient light reaching down to them. Sydney was glad they weren't driving through the canyon at night.

So he wants to get to know more about me, she thought, looking for a distraction to her dark thoughts. *He's going to have to ask, then.*

"Are you from Plymouth Falls originally?" she asked, deciding that now was as good a time as any to learn more about him.

A bit too late if he's an axe-murderer, though. Kind of hard to run when you're driving along at seventy miles an hour in a car with him.

"Born and raised," he said proudly, puffing up his chest. "Lived here all forty-four years. It's home."

"Forty-four?" she echoed, surprised at how much older than her he was. "You don't look it at all!"

"Why, how old are you?"

Sydney held back a grin as almost immediately Chief began falling all over himself telling her she didn't have to answer, that he hadn't been thinking, was too focused on the road, and half a dozen other excuses before she hushed him down.

"It's fine," she said, only now letting herself laugh.

Except it came out as a mirth-filled giggle. Not a normal

laugh, but a giggle. Chief's attention wavered from the road as he looked over at her, warmth filling his eyes. Oh dear, what had she done?

"It's fine," she repeated. "I'm thirty-five. I just thought you were closer to my age, that's all."

"Are you…are you bothered by the age difference?" he asked, a sudden, uncharacteristic nervousness entering his voice.

Judging by the reaction on his face, she wasn't the only one surprised to hear him sound so unsure of himself. Chief blinked furiously before adjusting his grip on the wheel, keeping those intense blue eyes of his facing the road, refusing to let her get a deeper look into them.

"Maybe if I was eighteen," she said lightly. "At this point in life, it doesn't really matter all that much, now does it? We're both adults…even if we acted like hormonal teenagers after a bit of booze."

Chief laughed, the loud, relieved sound filling the SUV, sending tingles across her arm. She liked hearing him laugh, she realized, though Sydney had no idea why that mattered all of a sudden.

More pregnancy hormones I suppose.

"It's amazing, isn't it," he said chattily. "When we first start drinking underage—which of course none of us *ever* did—we have no tolerance. Then we spend years building it up so we can act slightly more like adults while drinking. Then we *become* adults, and we no longer drink, so we act like teenagers while drinking again. That," he pronounced with a stab of a finger at the wheel. "That right there is the circle of life if I've ever heard it."

Sydney was laughing so hard by this point she had to

hold her stomach, bending over in the middle as she gasped for breath. It wasn't so much the concept, but his delivery of it, the sheer frustration in his voice, that had her in fits.

"I take it you know exactly what I mean?"

She sat back in the chair, nodding her head. "Yep. Completely. They always told me to fear teenage pregnancy. Nobody ever warned me about being stupid in my thirties and getting pregnant then." Her mood darkened. "They just always assumed by this point we would all want children anyway."

Until then, they had mostly avoided talking about their child. *Their child*. What a crazy concept and pair of words to be thinking about. She still wasn't quite ready to accept it, even as her right hand absently rubbed her stomach. Sydney was still far too early to begin showing, but the instinctive nature of the movement scared her terribly.

Chief had been great about not mentioning it. He'd simply called the trip 'the trip'. No mention of babymoon. No teasing about her eating for two. Nothing. Not only had he avoided mentioning it, but he'd done so in a manner that was so smooth she hadn't even *noticed* until just now, when she brought it up.

"Sorry," he mumbled. "I didn't mean for it to devolve into this. I wanted this trip to be about relaxation, and us learning to coexist together so that you maybe stop telling me to go away and not come back," he said sheepishly. "But I was hoping to do it naturally."

"It's fine," she said, almost reaching over to pat him on the shoulder.

Almost. Sydney didn't trust herself not to be able to do that and stop. She recalled how his muscles had felt under her fingers. It was too tempting to let her hand linger there, she had to keep her distance.

"Are you sure?"

"I'm positive," she said, looking around for a distraction, any distraction. "Where are we anyway? What is this place?"

Chief perked up as he glanced around. "Ah, well, you see that outcropping of rock over there?" He pointed until she nodded. "Well that is called Lion's Peak, and if you climb it at night during the new moon and face due north, you can see…"

Sydney smiled and leaned back into her seat, letting Chief fill her brain with knowledge once more. It was a comfortable routine by this point. One she could lose herself in, and forget the rest of the world. Which was exactly what she wanted to do.

Forget the world. And forget the situation she'd gotten herself into.

CHAPTER 9

Night fell, and with it Sydney slipped into sleep while he drove on.

So far she hadn't questioned his stamina for driving. Sydney had volunteered to drive several times, but she didn't fight him when he told her he was fine to continue. She was being polite, but was content to let him do the work. After all, he was the only one who knew their destination.

Their *real* destination. He hoped she would forgive him for the misdirection, but the two of them travelling together was *much* better cover than going it alone. He doubted the Tyrant-King had any spies along this desolate stretch of highway, but a man and a woman travelling together aroused no real suspicion. Most just ignored them and went about their lives.

A solo man of his size, however, would leave an impression upon many.

He drove carefully, fully aware of the precious cargo

encased in the seat next to him. Sydney had drifted off over an hour ago, after it had grown too dark for him to really point out any more landmarks. He smiled to himself, happy that she was enjoying the guided tour he was providing.

Chief had spent a lot of time studying up on the route, and then refreshing his memory again last night while she slept, so that he could demonstrate his knowledge to her and hopefully make the trip more interesting. So far it seemed to be paying off.

With the high beams on he took them around another corner. They would officially enter the mountains tomorrow afternoon, he estimated, and depending on the speed they made, they would arrive at their destination later that evening, or if they were forced to stop, the next morning. Chief was still debating that.

Entering during the morning would probably be for the better. He didn't want to alarm anyone, or wake anyone up. That would likely prove detrimental to what was already going to be a tough negotiation.

Not to mention it was going to be awkward enough explaining everything to Sydney. Being able to do so in daylight would probably be for the best. Maybe he could convince the Pacific pack to rent them a cabin, like the one she'd confessed to have been dreaming about. At least then he could prevent the trip from being a total disappointment to her.

A pair of eyes gleamed up ahead, caught in his headlights, and a second later the creature attached to them flung itself off the road a split second before Chief could get a good look at it. His foot was already on the brake pedal however, and the car slowed abruptly, jerking him and Sydney both forward against their seatbelts.

She stirred. "Everything okay?"

"Everything is fine," he said, replaying the scene in his mind. Had he really seen what he thought he saw? It couldn't be, though...out here? They were much too far from Pacific territory. Must have been a deer, his eyes just playing tricks on him. Or maybe a real wolf. They did still exist.

That made much more sense, in fact.

"Where are we?" Sydney asked sleepily, covering a yawn.

He smiled at the way her eyes crinkled up as she shook herself slightly throughout the process. It was the cutest way to yawn he could remember seeing on anyone.

"About half a day's drive from the mountains. We'll drive for another hour, there's a town up there."

"Okay." She yawned again in that same cute little manner. "What was with the sudden stop?"

"Animal on the road," he said, looking over to smile at her, reassure her that everything was okay. "Nothing to worry—"

There was a loud *bang* and the car started to swerve violently. It went off the road to the right, the front slamming into the near vertical slope of earth before rebounding off, careening across the median, spinning around twice and slamming driver-side on into the solid rock on the other side of the road, shattering his window and covering him in a dozen cuts.

The car came to a halt, engine still running, steam or

some kind of smoke sizzling up from the engine as they sat there, dazed by the sudden turn of events.

"Sydney!" Chief hissed, coming to his senses swiftly, looking over at her, violently clawing away the deployed airbags to get at her, concern rising. "Sydney!"

"I'm okay," she moaned. "My shoulder hurts from the seatbelt, but I'm okay. I think," she added with a hiss.

"We need to get out of the vehicle," he said, looking at the road.

They were on a blind left turn. Any oncoming car would come around and potentially hit them. It was the worst place to have an accident. They were going right through a cut in solid rock. The shoulder was perhaps two feet wide at best, then solid rock going up at a slope that was easily approaching ninety degrees. There was no room to maneuver.

"My door won't open," Sydney said, panic rising in her voice as she pulled on the handle and shoved over and over again.

"It's okay. It's okay," he repeated, eyes darting around the interior. "Just stay calm. Take the blanket, cover your head, okay?"

She did as she was told. With her face protected, Chief casually reached over and ripped her seatbelt free, and his as well. Unencumbered by that, he punched his way free of the windshield, the giant rectangular panel coming out as one piece. He had assumed the safety glass would do its job, but Chief wasn't about to risk Sydney's safety over an assumption.

He'd done that once already.

"Okay, come on, give me your hand," he said, reaching

in and carefully but firmly pulling her free of the wrecked SUV. The instant she was free of the enclosure he scooped her up into his arms and, after a brief visual check for oncoming headlights, darted across to the other side of the road.

"Is this much safer?" she asked, huddling deep into the blanket and leaning back against the rock.

The little bit of light from the SUV's headlights showed him that her eyes were unusually focused. Chief had expected her to be in more shock than this, but Sydney seemed to be processing everything just fine. Which meant she would be okay, much to his relief.

"Not really, but a little. I need to get some supplies out of the car before we go hiking."

"Hiking?" she all but yelped. "What do you mean hiking? Why don't you just call for help?"

"No signal," he said, pulling out his phone, pointing at it. "We need to get out of these hills first. We're too deep into them. There's a village just on the far side of the hills. It was my backup spot to stay. We'll be there in less than an hour, and we can get help then. Can you make it?"

Sydney just shook her head and laughed bitterly. "This is *really* not how I envisioned this trip going."

"If it makes you feel any better," he said, raising his voice as he jogged back across the highway and forced the trunk open, "it's not how I imagined it either."

Pulling out his backpack, he strapped it on, then snagged her bag, glad she'd used a duffel bag instead of a hard-shell suitcase. He could easily carry both.

"What the hell did you put in there?" she asked, eying his pack.

"It's all I had," he confessed, which was actually the truth. He'd not had *anything*, but he'd managed to borrow this from one of the other neighbors on the farm. It was what he'd wanted all along. Perfect, in case they couldn't drive all the way up to Pacific territory.

"Come on," he rumbled, and they set off. He left the lights on, hoping they would serve as a warning to anyone coming along. As soon as he could get signal on his phone he would have a tow truck come up to remove it, but for now, he didn't have much of a choice. Pushing it out of the way on his own would reveal a little too much to Sydney, and that wasn't a risk he could take.

"Can I ask you something?" Sydney said nearly half an hour later, the blanket pulled tight around her shoulders.

She'd remained silent until that point, and her sudden desire to talk meant he would have done just about anything to keep her going.

"Of course," he said, rubbing at his shoulder.

"Why didn't you just let the rock stop us when we first hit it?" she asked.

"What do you mean?"

"I saw you. You wrenched the wheel away, and you stopped us from spinning so that *your* side would take the next impact."

Chief frowned. How had she spotted that when it happened so quickly? He'd figured she would have been too caught up in the danger to notice. Apparently he wasn't giving her enough credit.

Rubbing the shoulder that had been hit by his door as it crumpled inward, Chief shrugged with the other. "Because you're carrying my child," he said, unable to tell her that he was also far better suited to deal with such impact. "I don't know why you hate that idea so much, or why you hate me for it, but you should know that I'll do anything to keep you safe."

Including bringing you on this trip to get you away from the war raging back home. Even if it means not giving you the babymoon of your dreams, that you deserve.

To his surprise Sydney reached out and laid a hand on his forearm. "Thank you," she said softly.

Chief just grunted, nodding his head, hoping she could see it in the dark. It would have to do. Just then he didn't trust his voice. The simple act of touching him had stolen it away. The soft, dainty pressure of her fingers on his skin. It was such a basic thing. Touch.

Yet it somehow rocked him to his core. Chief wasn't prepared for the intensity of his reaction to her, finding himself leaning in toward her before he could catch himself. "It was nothing," he said gruffly, pulling back, forcing distance between them, even as her fingers slipped from his arm with aching slowness. God, he wanted them back. "Just doing my job."

"Well, at your next performance review I'll make sure to keep that in mind," Sydney teased, then resumed walking. "Come on, let's go. I'm getting tired."

Chief smiled after her as she started hiking again. It wasn't just watching the curves of her body under the tightly wrapped blanket that had him smiling, though watching her hips move freely from side to side *was* mesmerizing in its own right. No, it was the slight warming of her attitude toward him that buoyed his spirits.

He'd been focused almost entirely on their unborn child

until now, determined to find a way to be involved with the pregnancy, so that he could help. If Sydney could learn to trust him, then maybe she would eventually come around to the idea of letting him raise the child himself, if she was still determined to believe she couldn't be a good mother.

Chief doubted he would be able to disabuse her of that notion, as silly as it seemed. There was something dark and powerful rooted inside her that was blocking Sydney from viewing the real her, and Chief wasn't sure he could be the one to fix it. He longed to, to free her from the bonds, to show her that she *did* have what it took to be a mother, but until he could defeat her demons for her, he knew that wouldn't come to pass.

So if he had to take the child on his own, he would. It would involve moving away from his pack. Living a life alone, where it was safe for him and his child. Maybe in time, if things were resolved, he could return, to show his child the halls of Moonshadow Manor, to have him or her walk the same corridors that Chief's parents, and their parents, had all walked.

In time. First, I have to get her to trust me.

Considering he'd lied to her about where they were going, it wasn't entirely wrong to say he was worried about that outcome. Chief would find a way to pull it off. Somehow. He had to. A lot of people were counting on him for it.

CHAPTER 10

"You're sure you don't have anything else?" Chief asked imploringly.

Sydney shook her head at his subtle insistence.

"I'm sorry sir, no. It's entirely unusual. Normally I would, but I've rented them all out," the proprietor apologized, though he declined to say why it was so unusual.

"It's fine," Sydney told him, shaking her head. "We'll take it," she said, leaning over the counter.

"I really am sorry. Just booked up yesterday for four days straight." The elderly man tugged on his unruly beard, looking back and forth between the two of them. "You're sure now?"

She nodded, then elbowed Chief so he would pay. "Yes, we'll be fine."

The man—his nametag read Harold—smiled in relief and pulled out a ledger. "If you'll just sign in," he said, pointing at the empty space.

Sydney tried not to laugh at the old-fashioned booking

system as she took up the pen and filled in her information with a flourish. "Not a problem."

The transaction complete, they headed down the row to their assigned room. Chief used the metal key to twist open the deadbolt and throw open the room.

"I bet you didn't expect this when we set out, did you?" Chief asked, pushing into the room with a troubled snort.

"Nope," she agreed, taking in the room.

It was old, but even as she looked around, Sydney had to admit it appeared well cared for. Everything was clean. The comforter was sharply pressed and hung neatly from the bed without any major wrinkles. The wallpaper was faded and the pattern mostly gone, but it wasn't peeling anywhere.

The carpet was worn down to nubs by now, but there were no visible stains, and even the corners appeared neatly vacuumed. Leaving her blanket on the bed, she went into the washroom.

"Oh my," she remarked in surprise.

Chief popped his head in just as she started to close the door. "Oh. Oh wow. That is something else."

The rose-pink tile job on the floor matched not just the shower, but the toilet as well. But the grout was clean and it wasn't stained or rusting. She had to give Harold credit. The man clearly couldn't afford to renovate, but he kept what he had clean as could be.

Once she was comfortable and had splashed some water on her face, Sydney collapsed onto the bed with an audible groan. Hiking had not been one of the advertised activities for the day, and after spending the better part of twenty-four hours in a car, she was *sore*.

"Everything okay up there?" Chief called from his spot on the floor.

"Just fine. Sorry about this," she mumbled, feeling guilty about taking the bed.

Not guilty enough to offer to share. Sydney was well aware of her weaknesses, and Chief with his muscles and toned stomach and wondrous cock was certainly up there. She had no doubt if they shared the single queen-sized bed in the room that things would get out of control between them.

"It's okay, I camp a lot. This is just like staying in a tent. Nicer, almost."

"Yeah." Sydney frowned. "I'm curious, though. Who told you that this sort of trip would be a good idea for a babymoon? Where on earth did you get that information from?" she finished with a laugh. "Because they got it so, so wrong."

Chief sat up. Rolling onto her side she saw he was looking at her with concern. "You're hating this right now, aren't you?"

She shrugged her free shoulder. "I mean, this sucks, but you didn't purposefully crash the car, so I can't exactly be mad at you for this, right?"

"No, I didn't," he confirmed with a wry smile. "But once we get there, I intend to try and make the best out of this, that I promise you."

"You know, Chief—and again I should have done this at the start—but I need to ask. *Where* is it we're going anyway?" Sydney was still trying to figure out what had prompted her to be so trusting of him on the issue. It wasn't like her, wasn't like her at all. Sydney *always* asked a ton of questions, and she never, ever, went anywhere with an effective stranger without knowing all the details first.

Unless his name is Lechiffre, apparently. Then I just lose all my instincts and agree to whatever he wants.

"You don't trust me," he said, sensing what she was saying.

"I don't know. I don't *know* you, Chief. I know nothing about you. You're all mystery and muscle, and for some reason I'm going along with that, when I really shouldn't be. For all I know you could be taking me to some mountain hideaway where you're going to chop me up into pieces."

"I would *never*!" he growled so loudly her skin vibrated from the sound. Then he relaxed, as if realizing what he'd done, and hurt filled his face. "Do you really think me capable of that sort of thing?"

Sydney shrugged. "I don't know *anything* you're capable of Chief. We had sex six weeks ago. I didn't see you again until a few days ago, now I'm in a car travelling across the country with you. This is crazy! I shouldn't be doing it. But I am, and I don't know why."

Maybe it wasn't her that Chief was after, she thought darkly. What if he didn't want the child after all? He could be taking her out to the middle of nowhere, where no one would ever find the body. They would never know his dark secret.

"I am not some sort of evil-doer," Chief promised.

Yet again, Sydney found herself wanting to believe him. There was simply too much earnestness in his voice. He was so honest and upfront, it was hard not to take everything he said at face value.

"I have your best interests in mind, I promise." He

flashed her what was probably supposed to be a disarming smile at that point, but Sydney went cold.

That was eerily close to something her parents used to say to her any time they did something she didn't like. *We're doing what's best for you.* The phrase echoed in her mind, she could almost see her mother sternly waving a finger at her as she said it.

"Sydney? What is it? What's wrong? What did I say?" Chief asked.

Ignoring him, she rolled over and pulled the blanket up. She didn't want to talk about it. Not to him. His trusting aura would have her spilling her life story in no time, and that wasn't something he needed to hear. She was thirty-five; an adult. Sydney would handle this on her own, like she always had. Even if it would be nice to have someone to trust.

But was Chief that person?

CHAPTER 11

Her clothes were gone. Scattered about the room when Chief had carelessly ripped them from her body. Literally ripped. She remembered the sound as he'd growled, pulling her collar apart as he stripped her of the rags of her shirt, tossing them behind him while he advanced.

Sydney's eyes had been too focused on his body to notice. He was naked except for his boxers, but they were so tight from the massive erection raging between his legs that they didn't leave anything to the imagination. She could see the outline of his cock as it strained at the sleek material, straining to be set free. Straining toward her.

And she wanted it, she realized, gasping as strong hands tore her jeans from her body, punctuated by yet another primal growl. Chief was about to take what he wanted: her. She was his, or would be, and Sydney had no resistance to give. Her body was on fire, aching for his touch. Everywhere his fingers or his mouth landed her body erupted in flame once more.

It was good. So good. She fell back with a yelp as Chief pushed her onto the bed, pulling her flimsy underwear to the side as his tongue dove deep, easily finding her clit with long, firm strokes. One hand slipped up her side and fingers closed around her ribcage, making Sydney feel tiny and small for the first time. In his hands, she *was* small.

His shoulders were so broad they pushed her legs apart, giving him easier access as he went at her with a hunger she didn't understand. What was it he saw in her?

Does it really matter?

Chief chose that moment to slip a finger inside her, pausing just inside the entrance. He was looking up at her now, she realized, everything a haze as her mind shut itself off, focused on one thing, and one thing only. Climax.

He brought her close with minimal effort, though her body was pulsing with need. Then a second finger worked its way inside her and in time with his tongue they curled upward, rubbing gently.

It was too much. She'd been on the edge, but the added sensation of something inside her...Sydney lost control and thrust into his face, warmth pouring out to envelop the rest of her body, holding it tight in a firm grip until the dam broke and she cried out. It was good, so good.

Chief stood up, and she frowned. At some point he'd lost his boxers. How was that possible? When had he had time to do that? And then he was at her entrance, pushing against her, a condom wrapped around his shaft. Chief hesitated, waiting for her nod, that one last confirmation that this was what she wanted.

She gave it.

He bent over her, taking her arms and pinning them to

her sides with casual ease, a thrill of electricity shooting through her body.

"Sydney," he growled, burying his face in her neck, nipping at the vein pulsing just below the surface. "Sydney."

"Chief," she moaned.

"Sydney."

"Chief."

"Sydney."

She frowned, confused. This was getting weird.

"Sydney."

Why wasn't he fucking her? Why was he saying her name over and over again?

"Sydney."

She jerked, eyes opening as the dream dissolved in front of her.

"Chief?" she asked, her mouth making a massacre of his name, still disoriented from her sudden awakening.

The dream went away, but the feeling didn't. Her body was on fire, aroused at the memory of their night of frenzied sex. Between her legs a dull ache pulsed out at slow, regular intervals. *Dammit.* She wanted him badly.

"What is it?" she asked. "Is something wrong?"

Chief shook his head, withdrawing his hand from her arm. That helped somewhat, but he was standing next to the bed, which meant his crotch was right at her eye level. He wasn't hard, like in her dream, but she knew what lurked below the dark blue denim.

"Nothing's wrong," he said. "I don't think. You were moaning and rolling around. I thought maybe you were having a nightmare," he said sheepishly.

"Oh. Yeah. Um. I was," she said, smiling broadly, wondering if it looked as awkward as it felt. "Thank you, for that. I'm much better now."

She tried to forget just how thoroughly turned on he could make her with little more than his touch. Even now part of her was tempted to kick back the covers and pull him down on top of her.

Stop that!

Kicking off the blanket—she'd never gotten dressed for bed she realized now—Sydney slipped past Chief and into the washroom, where she quickly splashed cold water on her face, extinguishing much—but not all—of the heat that had been threatening to take her over.

"Keep it together," she muttered, looking at herself in the mirror, short hair all a mess.

"What was that?" Chief called.

"Nothing," she said. "Nothing at all."

"Okay, well, don't take too long. We need to get a move on." He poked his head in the open door with a smile. It frowned as he looked around. "Ugh, this bathroom color gives me a headache." Then he was gone.

"Why the rush?" she asked, brushing her teeth with supplies from the kit in her duffel bag. "I thought we were on vacation."

"No, not quite," he said playfully. "We're on our *way* to vacation."

"Of course. How could I forget," she muttered through the toothpaste. "Suffering *before* enjoyment."

Chief laughed, but didn't respond, leaving her to her thoughts as she looked at bloodshot brown eyes set in the middle of a face covered in pale skin and freckles the color of her eyes. Freckles that were *all* over.

For most of her youth Sydney had considered them a curse. At one point she'd even learned to apply makeup to try and hide them. Then one year she'd just stopped caring what anyone else said. She looked the way she looked. They could either take it, or leave it.

Turns out most people left it. And her.

Not Chief, though. He'd come back for more after she'd told him about their child. Come back for more in a big way. *So why does it make me so angry that I can't stop thinking of him?*

The answer, she realized, was because right now all her thoughts of him were sexual. Not as a potential father, or a person. She just kept thinking about the way he felt close to her. Against her. Inside her. Even now she was burning up again after having a sex dream about him. It just wouldn't go away. She had so many more important things to be thinking about. She was pregnant! So why couldn't she stop thinking about his dick?

Sydney closed the door. The cold water on the face wasn't doing it. She needed a cold shower to get her brain sorted out, and she needed it soon. This couldn't go on.

Towel *extra* carefully tucked under her armpit, Sydney exited the washroom to grab some new clothes. She'd not thought about showering when she'd fled into its confines at first, and everything was still in her bag.

The instant she stepped through the door and the cloud

of steam dissipated—the cold shower had turned hot after she'd dumped water on the fire within her—she was hit with the smell.

"What is *that*?" she half-moaned, eyes darting over to a bag on the nightstand. "It smells so good!"

"Turns out there was a diner just down the road," Chief remarked. "I went and got us some breakfast while you were showering. Figured it would be the nice thing."

She smiled, pulling open a tin-foil wrapper to look upon the glorious food within. A fresh looking bagel topped with egg, cheese, tomato, bacon, lettuce. Her teeth dug in and flavor flooded her mouth. Sydney moaned, not caring how it looked or sounded as she sat on the edge of the bed, desperately holding on to a towel that was threatening to fall down to her waist while she scarfed down the delicious food. At some point she'd grown hungry without realizing it.

"Thank you," she said around the food, tasting the sharp cheddar. This was no cold motel breakfast of almost-stale cereal and milk. No, this was heaven in circular form.

"Not a problem. There's more in there, take your time. You can eat in the car too."

Sydney perked up. "The car?"

Chief nodded. "Yeah, Harold put me in contact with a local mechanic. Came out here early this morning, we got everything sorted."

Narrowing her eyes, Sydney took another bite, this time noting the crispiness of the thick bacon. "There can't be a rental car agency here in town," she countered. "This place is far too small for that sort of thing."

"No, but there is a dealership."

"What? You just *bought* a new car?" she yelped, bits of food falling from her mouth, some of them embarrassingly dropping between her towel-cleavage.

"It's fine," he assured her, his face twitching as she dug between her breasts to retrieve bits of cheese, bacon and bagel. "Need a hand?"

She glared at him.

"Sorry! Sorry," he laughed. "I couldn't resist."

"Yeah well, we all know what happened the last time neither of us resisted," she muttered.

Standing, Chief's face turned to granite almost immediately.

"Wait, Chief," she said; pleaded.

"I'll be outside," he ground out, leaving the room, and her.

Sydney groaned. Why had she said that? In what world was that a nice thing to say?

Great. All he does is be nice to you, and then you throw that in his face. Enjoy spending the day sitting next to him in a car. That won't be awkward at all!

CHAPTER 12

Well this is awkward.

Chief tapped his fingers lightly against the steering wheel in time with the tune on the radio. He didn't know the words, but the beat was catchy and it even had him bobbing his head along to it. Something about a blank space and a woman pretending to be a man's perfect catch until she had him. It was all gibberish, but it was a welcome distraction from Sydney.

Then again, anything was a welcome distraction from her just then. Stone-faced and silent, she'd sat in the passenger seat without a word since he'd left the hotel. It was the most uncomfortable drive quite possibly of his life. She didn't say a word, only getting out when he stopped for gas, using the restroom and then returning to her seat. Eyes forward, hands folded in her lap.

She didn't even sleep. That, perhaps, was the weirdest part to her behavior. Both days prior she'd fallen asleep multiple times while he drove. Not today, though. Today she stayed wide awake.

At first he'd let her have her silence, letting his anger at her comment simmer within him, but eventually it had gone out. Keeping an anger going for long periods of time wasn't exactly his specialty, and with Sydney it flamed out faster than he'd expected. Now all he wanted was to talk to her.

But now it seemed like she, was pissed at *him*, and how was *that* fair? Was his one comment really worth this cold shoulder attitude that he was getting? They needed to talk bluntly about the subject at hand, he could tell that now. Chief had thought things were progressing between them, but apparently he'd been wrong.

"I'm sorry."

Chief was so lost in his thoughts that he barely even heard the nearly whispered apology. "Pardon?" he asked. "Sorry for what?"

"Earlier. My comment, it was out of line."

He chewed on that for a moment. Had her silence been something other than anger? A quick sidelong glance showed that her face was slightly red. Had she been *embarrassed* about snapping at him? Was this born of guilt? Perhaps, he decided.

"So was mine," he told her, deciding against pushing the subject. "It was a poor joke that I should have known wasn't welcome."

"Maybe," she agreed. "But I shouldn't have responded the way I did."

"Even?" he asked, sticking out his right hand.

"Even," she agreed, taking it.

They shook once while he drove with his left, and a sudden gust of wind forced him to grip the wheel a little harder to keep the car going straight. In response, the fingers of his right hand tightened around Sydney's hand as well.

He was about to apologize and pull his hand back, when to his surprise she just let the clasped hands down to rest on her knee, attention returning to the landscape ahead of them.

"It might not be flying first class and staying at the Ritz," she said slowly, "but I have to admit, the view is stunning no matter what."

Ahead of them, the mountains rose high into the air. They were close enough now that Chief would have to lean way forward to see the top of them, the peaks hidden by the roof of the car as the earthen titans reached forward to swallow their tiny vehicle among them.

In the distance the snow-capped tops of some of the taller peaks were visible, wreathed in clouds. It was a beautiful sight, and one that stole his breath for several minutes as well. Thy drove on in silence, hand in hand, neither speaking, neither moving, simply appreciating nature for its beauty.

And then, just like that, the highway dove between two stone giants, and they were in the mountains. The journey was almost over. They would stop early in another hour or so, and then make the rest of their trip tomorrow morning he decided. Their destination wasn't far, but Chief decided he wanted to take her exploring first.

Risking a glance over at Sydney he saw the wonder in her eyes, the slight slackening in her jaw as she leaned forward to see it all. The Rockies truly were stunning, but Chief knew that to really appreciate it, he needed to take her hiking in them.

"Thank you," she said softly. "This is just beautiful, Chief. I've never seen anything like them before."

He smiled. "You're welcome. I'm glad you're enjoying it."

"I didn't believe you at first," she admitted. "But I do now."

Chief almost bit his lip, keeping the next comment from slipping out, but he didn't. "You should believe me more often," he said, squeezing the hand he still held. "I'm not such a bad guy."

She laughed. "I don't think you're a bad guy! I'm sorry if I ever gave you that impression."

He shrugged. "Not really. I mean, when you came over to yell at me the other day, maybe, but I think we're past that now."

Sydney winced. "Sorry. I was just...I thought you'd lied to me, and then dealing with the shock of this situation. I wasn't very nice. You didn't deserve that. I should have handled it better."

"Maybe," Chief admitted. "But this is a big deal, you know. For *both* of us." He tried to stress that part. "We're in this together, Sydney. You need to know that. It's not you against the world. I'm here for you. For both of you. Let me in, and I can help. A shoulder, a hand, a hug, a midnight pickles and ice cream fetcher. Whatever it is, *I can help*."

He left the last part unspoken. *If you let me.*

Sydney closed down, pulling her hand away as she crossed her arms, not looking over at him. Chief watched, trying to ignore how empty and cool his hand felt without hers in it. He didn't need that distraction.

"I know," she said at last, breaking the silence. "I really do, Chief. I really do. It's just not that easy."

It is! he wanted to scream at her; to shake her by the shoulders until she woke up and realized that yes, it was that easy. That simple. Just let him in, let him help. Why wouldn't she do that? Why was Sydney so unwilling to accept that he wanted to be there for her and the child?

"I want to help. The entire time. I can't grow the baby," he admitted with a rueful laugh, watching a ghost of a smile play across her face. "But while you're pregnant, whatever you need I can get it. And after…"

Her face grew clouded. "After, I'm giving it up for adoption. Remember?"

"I remember you said that, yes." Chief didn't like the way their tones were becoming colder, more distant toward one another. "I want to be this child's father, Sydney. That's *important* to me."

"Sending it to a home where it will be properly loved and looked after is important to me," she countered. "Living on a farm with twenty other partiers and reckless people is not a good family life, Chief. No matter how you skin it, that's not the life a child needs or deserves. No, a good family will take it, and raise it, and that's that."

Chief's knuckles tightened around the steering wheel as he worked to contain his anger. This wasn't her choice. It *couldn't* be her choice. Could it? Chief had no idea how the law worked when it came down to these things, but it had to give him some rights as the father, didn't it? Who else was better suited if the mother couldn't handle it?

The father who is a wolf shifter living in near-constant danger of being killed by those he's rebelling against.

Sydney had a point there, he knew, but that was why he would leave. His pack would support him. He'd yet to ask, but some things just went without saying of course. Chief could *do* this alone.

But he found he didn't want to. Not entirely. He wanted Sydney to be there, he realized. For the two of them to tackle this together. As it should be. Yet for some reason she wanted absolutely nothing to do with this child. Why? There was something she was hiding, something Sydney wasn't telling him.

"Have you talked to your parents about this at all?" he asked, trying another avenue of approach. Anything that would let him in, past her defenses even just a little bit.

If it was possible her face grew darker. "Ha!" she barked. "No, I know that this is what's right."

Chief shook his head, the panoramic landscape around them forgotten. "How?" he pressed. "How do you know that giving it up to some random family is better than me, the biological father, raising it?"

"Because," she snapped. "It just is, okay?" She looked away, staring out her side window, forcing Chief to talk to the back of her head.

He found himself forced to rein in his temper, the fuse burning hotly.

"That makes no sense," he growled, fingers gripping the wheel even tighter.

"I'm pregnant, I don't have to make any sense!" she said with more than a hint of bitterness.

Explosive, sarcastic laughter erupted from his chest.

"Seriously? That's the card you're playing? You're six weeks pregnant, Sydney. Get real."

Her head whipped around like it was on a swivel, brown eyes boring into him, burning with the light of a thousand suns.

Shouldn't have said that. I should not have said that.

"You have a lot to learn," Sydney hissed, a lock of her short brown hair falling across part of her forehead and partially obscuring one eye, giving her a slightly maniacal angry gleam to the look she turned on him.

Then her back was to him once more.

Chief wanted to groan. Mere minutes ago they had been holding hands and he'd felt closer to her than ever.

Now he was pretty sure she was thinking of ways to kill him in his sleep.

What *else* was going to go wrong on this trip?

CHAPTER 13

Sydney knew that her thoughts were irrational. Yet she was having them anyway.

Just like you're having the child anyway.

Of course she was having the child. It was growing inside of her now. That was one thing. She could do what it took for nine months to grow one. That strength was something she possessed. It was after that, the actual *raising* of the child. That was where Sydney would be a failure, and that was why it needed to go to a family better suited to provide such an upbringing.

Every child deserved to have what she hadn't. What she couldn't give, either. It was as simple as that. Chief wasn't that person. He was too flawed, and his living situation had *all kinds* of red flags about it. There was somewhere north of twenty men living on that farm, all of them tall, all of them slathered in muscle.

And none of them knew a damn thing about farming, either. Chief thought she didn't know, but it was clear to her that they were up to something else there. Something he wasn't telling her about. Whatever it was, she doubted it was any good, and there was no way in hell a child of hers was being raised by a gang of criminals.

Come on now. Chief isn't a criminal.

Maybe not, she was forced to admit to herself. And he did mean well. She could see that it hurt him to hear her say she was putting the child up for adoption, but to Sydney's mind, she had no other choice. She wasn't cut out for this, why couldn't he see that?

"I can be a good parent," Chief said quietly after some time had passed.

"Chief, you're living a lie," she said bluntly.

"Excuse me?" he snapped, rearing back. "What gives you the right to judge me on how good of a parent I could be? You don't know me."

"Exactly!" she hissed. "That's exactly it. I *don't* know you, Chief."

Yet I got in a car and drove across the country, with you as my only way home. What the hell was I thinking?!

"What do you mean?" His voice was calmer, more relaxed. "What do you want to know?"

She sighed. "I hate it when you do that."

"Do what?"

"Go from angry to calm and rational in an eyeblink. It's hard to stay angry at you." She remained facing forward, not able to look over at him.

"I don't want you to be angry with me at all," he admitted. "It hurts me that you get that way. I just want to be good. For you."

Something shivered through her at the way he said that.

The emphasis on her. It was strong. Was she reading too much into that? What was he trying to say?

"Then tell me what it is you're really doing on that farm," she said, testing him.

"What do you mean?'

Sydney didn't bother to hold back her sigh of frustration. "I'm not an idiot, Chief. Not a one of you is a farmer. On top of that, it's basically like an all you can eat muscle buffet. Every one of you is six and a half feet tall. You're all gorgeous— What?"

Chief shook his head, jaw tight, eyes still radiating that sudden burst of fury that had caused her to stop talking. "Nothing," he said through clenched teeth. "Go on."

"Okay," she said, dragging the word out, making it clear she knew he was full of shit. Did he not like it when she said that the other guys on the farm were hot? *Too bad, buster, you don't have the only claim on that, even if I know what those hands can do, and how firm those arms feel when they— Down girl!*

Clearing her throat, Sydney continued. "You all look like you're made from the same mold, then painted somewhat differently," she said. "It doesn't take a genius to realize the farm is basically a meathead convention in the country. There's nothing natural about it."

"I'm all natural," he protested.

"Not what I meant," she groaned, shaking her head. "And you know it. So stop treating me like I'm some oblivious airhead. Especially since none of you ever talk about farming. I've only been over a few times, but the conversations are all guarded, and the bits I *do* hear about sound more...I don't know, almost military, in nature." She paused, then stared directly at him. "Are you some sort of mercenary group hiding out?"

Chief blinked, his face impossible to read. It didn't react to her question. If it weren't for his eyes, she'd assume he was some sort of marble statue, so impassive did he gaze back at her.

"No."

"How forthcoming of you," she said without missing a beat, ignoring the gravity he'd tried to impart on that one word. "You see, though? You're not telling me the truth, Chief, and it's obvious!"

"Neither are you," he fired back. "You keep telling me this is all about the better life for our child, but we both know it's not just that. You're hiding something from me, so don't act all high and mighty."

"So what?" she practically shouted. "Maybe that's *why* I'm saying the child will be better off with another family."

"*Our* child will be better off with its parents," Chief stressed.

"Nobody would be better off with you!"

They *were* shouting now, as tempers flared and got the better of them after two and a half long days locked in a small vehicle together.

"At least I can face reality and accept that this is happening," he fired back angrily. "You won't even acknowledge that we're having a child. We're going to be parents whether you're scared of it or not."

"I am not scared!" she screamed. Why couldn't he just come around to her way of thinking? It would be so much easier this way!

"You are too. You're freaking out over something natural and normal."

"Because I didn't want this! I was happy the way I was, and then you came along—"

Chief cut her off. "And *what*?" he sneered. "Rocked your world? You had every chance to go home alone, but you wanted *me* as much as I wanted you. We did this together, and you need to get over yourself and stop blaming your decisions on me, simply because something unexpected happened."

"Oh please," she snorted. "You weren't *that* good. Why I—"

She never completed her sentence. A black four-door sedan came out of nowhere and nearly cut them off as it passed, forcing Chief to pull the car to the right slightly and slow down abruptly. The near-miss stole her breath, and they both lapsed into silence, living in their own minds for the moment.

CHAPTER 14

The silence was a welcome relief.

After his heart slowed at the unexpected near collision, Chief dedicated most of his focus to the road around him. He was the one in the driver's seat, and it was his job to be responsible for all three of them. By letting his emotions get the better of him he'd failed to notice the car overtaking them at a reckless pace, and it had nearly resulted in them crashing.

That was his fault, and he simmered in shame for it now, his eyes constantly flickering between the rear view mirror and the road ahead of them. It wouldn't happen again, that was for certain. Nor would he allow himself to get so heated with her.

It was a touchy subject, and Chief didn't blame Sydney for being upset about it at all. That was completely and thoroughly understandable of course. This was a huge, life-changing experience that had been thrust upon them without their consent or expectation.

The difference was that Chief was more interested in that path, while Sydney seemed to be okay with living her life alone, and without children. To her, he could understand, this might seem like it was ruining her life. Hopefully she would come around. A few weeks wasn't much time to adjust her entire outlook to the changes coming. He might just need to give her time.

And you're going to have to come up with an explanation for what you and the others are doing on the farm as well. She isn't going to buy anything that isn't believable.

Which certainly excluded the truth. Oddly, though, the idea of lying to Sydney, of telling her something that would assuage her concerns, didn't appeal to him in the slightest. In fact, even considering it was rubbing him the wrong way. He wanted to be open and honest with her. Completely. But he couldn't tell her the truth. No way.

He was going to have to come up with something, however, and soon, because Chief had yet to tell her about their true destination, and bringing her among another pack was only going to arouse more questions, not fewer.

They were nearing Pacific territory as well. The road was mostly empty by this point, which was why the car coming out of nowhere had startled both of them so badly. Something about that bothered him. Why had they felt the need to cut it so close when passing?

Motion in the rear view mirror caught his attention as another black sedan roared up behind them. Chief pulled over slightly in his lane, making it easier for them to pass. The headlights grew brighter in the late afternoon light. Something wasn't right here.

The car behind wasn't moving to go around them.

"Hold on," he growled, suddenly punching the accelerator.

Both he and Sydney were pushed back into their seats as the large four-door picked up speed. He wished fervently that they were still in the SUV they'd set out in. It was a former House Canis vehicle that had been stolen on one of their raids, the GPS disabled. It was reinforced, with a souped up engine and other goodies available to him. The six-year-old not-quite-luxury sedan was anything but.

"Chief, what's going on?" Sydney asked, craning her head around, trying to look behind them. "Who are they?"

He didn't get a chance to answer. Their pursuer was too fast, and the car slammed into their rear end with a shriek of tortured metal. A second later, the smell of burnt rubber reached their noses as the car turned slightly sideways, the wheels smoking as the car behind them tried to spin them out.

Chief wasn't having any of that, however, and he whipped the wheel around while applying the brakes, then hit the gas once more. The sudden half-spin stop-and-go threw their pursuer off, and the vehicle began to gain distance.

"Chief! What the hell is going on? Why are they trying to hit us?" Sydney shouted.

"I don't know," he growled. "Now let me focus."

It was true, he didn't know. But he had his suspicions.

The Pacific pack didn't want them among their territory. How they had found out it was him, Chief didn't know. It wasn't like they'd called ahead to announce he was coming. Things didn't quite work that way. Pacific liked their privacy. That was why they lived mostly off the grid.

Now they were showing him the hard way what happened to those who trespassed.

"I don't think we're getting away," he pronounced as the car behind them picked up speed, gaining on them courtesy of its better acceleration.

"Okay. What does that mean?" she asked.

"It means we're going to crash," he answered, swerving back and forth, avoiding the attempted ram each time. "I think," he added, eyes lighting up as he saw something coming up ahead.

"What?" Sydney asked, picking up on his tone. "What is it?"

"Might be a hope," he said hurriedly, glancing in the mirror. He would have to time it just right. "If we do crash, try to stay limp. Tensing up will only make it worse."

"Right. Yeah. Totally relaxed. That's definitely doable right now," she muttered sarcastically.

"I'm trying to help," he said, irritated.

"Sorry. You're right. Drive," she encouraged.

Up ahead the road widened as a service road appeared on their right, leading steeply up the mountainside. Chief steered slightly toward it, hoping the pursuers would take the bait.

They did, gunning their acceleration, pulling up on his inside, trying to cut him off, forcing him to stay on the highway. As they did, Chief stomped on the brakes.

The abrupt loss of speed caught their pursuers by surprise, and their vehicle shot forward, until *it* was in front of him.

"Gotcha," Chief snarled, wrenching the wheel to the

right, slamming the nose of his vehicle into the rear of the black sedan.

It almost worked as planned. Almost. Chief had forgotten one key thing. The difference in road elements. By turning to the right, his front wheels left asphalt and went onto the dirt of the service road as it started to peel away in a Y-shape. The different traction whipped their vehicle around, spinning them wildly out of control.

"We're gonna make it!" he shouted as they crashed through the service entrance.

And hit a pothole. A *big* pothole.

The sudden impact, combined with the spinning, flipped the car on its roof, the metal howling with impacts as it was shredded by the gravel of the road as they slid uncontrollably across the service road with nothing to stop them.

CHAPTER 15

The horrendous sound against the roof continued as they went, the car slowly shedding speed. They didn't slow fast enough, because the car went over the edge of the road and slide down the embankment. They came to a jarring, but not overly painful halt against a pair of trees. Metal crunched and at least one of the windows broke.

But they were alive.

Chief ripped off his seatbelt immediately. He hadn't seen what happened to their pursuers, but he knew that their status could change in a heartbeat if he didn't do something about it. His focus couldn't be on their car. Not for long. There were too many external dangers out there.

With his seatbelt out of the way, he slumped to the ground awkwardly, his legs still pointing into the air.

"We need to get out of the car," he said, grabbing Sydney's flailing arms and holding them still. "We're alive. Pull yourself together. There's no time for you to freak out."

"I think freaking out is perfectly natural in this

moment," she shouted as he tried to grab at her seatbelt. She pushed him away. "What are you doing?"

"Getting you out of here," he growled, casually ripping the seatbelt free. Now wasn't the time to worry about questions of his strength and abilities. Now was the time to get her out of the vehicle and to safety. There wouldn't be much time.

His arms caught her shoulders, and together they awkwardly lowered and turned Sydney until she was in a crouched position on the cars roof. Satisfied that for the moment she wasn't in trouble, Chief pulled back a leg and with all the strength he possessed, slammed it into the door.

The metal protested, but a second kick nearer the hinge sent the panel spinning away from the car. He crawled out, turned and hoisted Sydney to her feet.

"Go into the trees," he said, pointing off to his left, facing her and the car. "Twenty feet. Wait there for me, okay? Do not go running off. Do you understand?"

"I'm terrified," she snapped. "Not stupid. I got it. Twenty feet. Wait for you." She frowned. "Where are you going?"

Chief turned to look for the other vehicle, but he couldn't spot it from where they were.

"I'm going to ensure whoever that is realizes they fucked up," he snarled, and practically leapt up the steep embankment, eyes searching for the tracks the other car made as it crashed.

Chief had no idea how badly the others might be hurt, but he had to strike and strike quickly if he was going to have any hope of keeping them out of harm's way. There would be more of them than him, and he needed to even the odds.

Racing along the gravel road he came across the other cars tracks, and also realized why he hadn't been able to see the black sedan from in the embankment.

Whereas his vehicle had almost lazily slid down on its roof, their attackers had basically launched themselves from the side of the road. The black sedan had skipped over some shorter trees and was practically embedded into the forest itself.

And the driver was getting out.

Chief growled and lunged at the man, taking them down in a heap. There was no time for niceties. The driver was reaching for a knife even as Chief hit him in the side. Whatever this was, they didn't intend on taking him alive.

The pair went down, and Chief snaked in behind, getting a firm grip on the drivers skull with both hands.

"Drop the knife," he threatened, turning the head at a sharp angle.

The driver glared up at him and his hand dove for the concealed weapon again.

Chief flexed and turned his body violently. Bone snapped, and the driver went limp in his arms.

"What a waste," he spat, getting up, ready for any other attackers.

But there were none. He frowned, positive he'd seen at least a second body in the car before the crash. Easing his head up he looked into the car, eyes scanning the interior.

Almost immediately he yanked his head back and turned away, nearly vomiting at the sight inside.

There *had* been other passengers. Two of them in

fact, one in the passenger seat and another directly behind him. Unfortunately for them, a thick tree branch had punched through the window, impaling both of them as the force of the impact turned it into a spear.

"What a way to go," he mumbled to himself, feeling terrible that his first reaction was one of relief. Nobody else was nearby.

There was a buzzing sound. Chief frowned, tracing it back to the pocket of the driver. He pulled it out. Two text messages. The first was unreadable unless he could unlock the phone, but the second was displayed.

We are en route to your position.

Chief straightened. *Okay brain, think. You got lucky. You're alive, but pursuit is coming. Neither vehicle is driveable. What do you do?*

As he was trying to come up with a plan, something caught his attention. It was the face of the driver, looking up at him empty-eyed, jaw slack. Chief had seen plenty of death before, so he wasn't fazed by that. No, it was the fact he *recognized* the man's face.

He wasn't a member of the Pacific. He was a guard, loyal to the Tyrant-King.

Which could only mean one thing: Chief had been followed. He glanced back at the phone. More of them were on the way as well. More loyalists. There would be no talking, no convincing them not to attack. They would come for him.

And Sydney.

He swore loudly. If they had been following him, that meant they'd seen him with Sydney. They knew she was someone to him. And they would use that against him. Ruthlessly.

That left only one unpleasant option. They were near Pacific territory. Perhaps three hours' drive along the highway. If they could make it there, perhaps Lenard, the Alpha, would grant them safety within his lands while Chief made his pitch for them to join the rebels cause.

It was a long shot, but he didn't see much of an option. They had to shake their pursuers, and the other vehicle— his mind shot back to the sedan that had cut them off earlier —would be along far before any tow truck or other sort of help.

Shit.

He jogged back to their car. "Sydney!" he called. "It's okay now."

She came out of the forest, concern on her face. "Chief what's going on?"

"I'll tell you later," he promised. There was no time for the details now. They had to get a move on. "Are you hurt at all?"

"Bruised," she admitted. "Shook up. But no, otherwise, I think I'm okay." Her eyes darted past him, up the road.

"They weren't as lucky," he said neutrally, hoping to keep it at that, without having to get into more detail. Nobody deserved to come upon that scene, but Chief couldn't worry about that, not now. His focus was Sydney. She was all that mattered.

"Chief," she said, interrupting his thoughts. "Chief there's no signal out here."

"I know," he said. That was part of the reason why the

Pacific liked it so much. It was extremely remote. No reason for humans to come this way except to go camping or hiking in the mountains. "Come on, though. We need to go."

Reaching into the front seat he pressed the button to pop the trunk. It opened partway, getting stuck on the ground. All their stuff tumbled down, but there wasn't enough space to get out.

Angrily Chief grabbed the flimsy metal and pulled down, ripping the trunk free. All their belongings spilled out. He took his pack and set it aside, along with the black bag he'd brought with them.

"What's in there?" she asked.

"Supplies."

Her eyebrows went up. "You expected his?"

"Not at all. But we are in the middle of nowhere. I believe in being prepared. There's a tent, ration bars, and a few other things that could come in handy."

He bent over the two bags, pulling things from his hiking pack, trying to make room, to condense it all down to one bag. The weight wasn't an issue, he could handle that. What he knew, however, was that Sydney was going to have to travel unencumbered if they had any hope of making it out alive. That meant packing light.

When he was done, Chief hoisted the pack up and settled it into place. "Right. Let's go then," he said.

There was no answer. Looking about wildly, he saw nothing. Sydney was gone.

"Sydney!" he called, climbing the embankment in two panicked leaps of supernatural strength.

He spied her then, the rust red of her hair a dead give-away among the black of the highway and the greenery around them.

"What are you doing?" he asked, jogging over to her quickly. "We need to go, come on." He tugged on her arm, heading back up the service area.

"I'm waiting for a car to come by, to give us help," she said, sounding dazed.

No, not now! The last thing he needed was for shock to begin setting in. Chief should have known it would. She'd been too calm after the crash, too composed. Now she was retreating back into her mind, unable to come to grips with the reality of their situation.

"Sydney, there's no time for this," he growled, taking her by the arms and guiding her back up the service road as fast as he could. "We need to go *now*, before it's too late."

CHAPTER 16

The comforting warmth of his arm around her shoulders eventually seeped through the hazy barrier that had risen up to swallow her while she waited in the forest. It was then that her brain had begun to realize what had just happened to them. How close to death the two of them had been. It was a major shock, and she'd not been able to cope.

Blinking rapidly to clear the last of it away, Sydney looked around in confusion. This wasn't the highway. Where were they?

The forest had closed in around them. Her legs burned slightly. Glancing behind she saw it was because they were headed uphill. Away from the highway. A *long* way away.

"Uhhh, Chief?" she said, looking around, trying to remember how she'd gotten there, but having no recollection of it. "Where are we?"

"Heading up the mountain," he said, not stopping. "We'll leave the road soon, take to the wilds. I can find us a game trail, we'll make decent time."

"Uh huh. Um, decent time to *where*?" she asked force-fully. "What's going on?"

"We need to keep moving," was all she got in response. That and a tug on her arm, pulling her farther up the service road. The end was just ahead, the gravel road terminating at a chain-link fence that wrapped around the base of a radio tower of some sort.

Sydney stumbled along another few hundred feet, pausing again as Chief took a sudden left, departing from the road and heading into the forest.

"Where are we going?" she repeated, intending to stand her ground.

Chief paused, turned around and came back up to her in several long strides, his powerful legs easily closing the distance, until he was looming up above her. Sydney was suddenly reminded not only of his huge size, but also that she barely knew this man, and now he was pulling her along into the forest, into the wild.

Where no one can find me.

"I told you. We're heading up the mountain. Now let's go, we don't have time to waste," he growled, blue eyes pale and cold.

"No!" she exclaimed, raising her voice. "I'm not going anywhere with you. Not until you explain what's going on, and why we're suddenly fleeing into the countryside!"

"Shhh," Chief hissed, his eyes darting back down the hill. "Keep it down."

"Don't tell me what to do! You don't own me Chief. Now tell me what's—mmm!"

Sydney glared, first at the fingers covering her mouth, then lifting her head to turn the angry look on the owner.

"Keep your voice down and I'll remove my hand. Okay?"

"Mmfg uuu!"

Chief's eyebrows came together. "Did you just say 'fuck you' to me?"

She nodded, letting out a whole string of words, trying to speak through his palm.

The big man blinked. "Sorry, I don't speak gibberish, and we don't have time for this playschool bullshit either, Sydney. This is serious."

She calmed slightly at the alarm in his tone. Something was bothering him.

"Ooot?" she said into his hand, shrugging her shoulders at the same time, then pointing back down the mountain.

"I'm assuming that means what." He sighed. "If I take my hand off your mouth, will you at least keep your voice down?"

She nodded, and he pulled his hand back.

"Tell me what the hell is going on, Chief, right now, or I swear to god me talking loud is going to be the least of your problems!" She let fury flow into her voice, uncaring of the size difference between them.

But she kept the decibel level down.

"We need to get into the mountains and lose ourselves," Chief said, routinely peering over her shoulder to watch the road behind her. "The men in that car, they aren't the only ones. More are coming. Soon. We need to lose ourselves in the forest, and find some water or something that I can use to cover our scent before they catch up."

Cover their scent? Were these men bringing hunting

dogs? Why were they after her? Or him? It had to be him. Were they the police?

"I can see you have questions," Chief said. "I'll answer them later, but right now we need to move fast. I won't be able to save us if we stay here and discuss things in a committee."

Sydney bristled. "I am *not* a committee!" But her voice was still low.

"Let's go then," Chief growled, and this time she left the road when he pulled on her arm, following him through the brush until he found a small trail that wound along the hill-side, taking them deep into the forest.

The sun reached its zenith and began to decline as they hiked. Sydney's legs burned from the unexpected and unaccustomed exertion, but she didn't complain. Mostly because she didn't have the breath to do so. Chief was setting a killer pace, though she was quite confident he was flustered at how slow they were going.

Some of his words finally penetrated to her thought-processing section of her brain, and Sydney finally found some breath to speak as they started going downhill instead of up for a little bit.

"Chief." She whispered his name, loath to break the silence that had enveloped them after they entered the wilderness of the mountainside.

He glanced back, lifting his eyebrows in question, but didn't speak.

"More of *who* are coming, Chief? And why are they after you?" She left it unsaid that it was obvious they weren't after her. Nobody was after her. "How many more?"

"More than I can handle," he rumbled quietly. "That's all I can be sure of."

They continued hiking. At one point a fallen log blocked their path. Instead of going around as she'd intended, Chief simply scooped her up into his arms and, casually holding her in place with one arm, climbed up and over the massive trunk, gently hopping down to the other side.

"Thanks," she mumbled, tugging her clothes back into place, trying to ignore the way they peeled from her skin, so dampened by sweat were they.

Chief just grunted and continued to lead the way.

"Can I ask you something?" she asked as they skirted a patch of dense brush that blocked their way.

"Mmm," came the answer. The *distracted* answer. Chief was focused on their path more than anything. His focus almost uncanny.

"This trip was never about a babymoon, was it?" she accused. "You're trying to run away from something, and you wanted me to come along, didn't you? Didn't want to leave me behind?"

Chief bristled. "I am *not* running away."

She scratched her temple, then wiped sweat away with the back of her hand. It just smeared it more. Yuck.

"So what do you call what we're doing right now?" she asked.

"Tactical repositioning?" he tried, speaking in a whisper.

Sydney just sighed.

"Okay, right now we're retreating to safety, yes. But this trip, was not me running away from something. If I were the type to do that," he said, spinning on her, pinning her to the leafy floor with a burning blue gaze, "then I would have left you behind."

He let his stare linger for a second or two, driving his point home, then returning to blazing a trail through the forest.

"So you confirm it then, this was never about the baby-moon," she added after he'd taken several steps.

Chief paused mid-step for a fraction of a second, then continued walking. But he didn't speak.

"That's what I thought," she muttered angrily, wishing now that she'd never left her farm. "You lied to me."

A ragged, pained noise filled the forest.

"Are you alright?" she asked, thinking that something had happened to Chief, rushing forward to come around to the front of him.

But he wasn't hurt, she realized almost instantly upon looking at his face. Not physically. "I'm sorry," he rasped, looking down, unable to meet her gaze. "I had—*have*—every intention of taking you somewhere. I do. It's just, there's something I need to do first."

"I knew it!" she hissed. "I knew it. Nobody drives across country for a babymoon. That's just ridiculous. But you and your blue eyes and big biceps made me forget about logic and trust you that this was for real." She smacked a fist into her palm loudly. "That's twice now I've made bad decisions because of your good looks. Never again, mister. Just know that!"

Chief was wincing, eyes darting around the forest, and Sydney realized her voice had crept up in level as she talked.

"Sorry," she said in a quiet voice. "I guess I'm just a little *furious* that you brought me along on this trip, putting me in danger, and I don't even get a vacation out of it."

His broad shoulders slumped. "Would you believe it if I told you I brought you along because I wanted to keep you safe?"

She snorted. "*This*," she said, waving around at the forest. "This is your version of safe?"

"Admittedly it's backfired colossally," he said with a weak shrug of his shoulders, palms facing upward. "I did not predict this would happen."

"No shit it's backfired," she said. "Does that at least mean you're going to finally explain to me what the hell is going on?"

"Not yet," Chief rumbled, his eyes looking around. "Let's go," he said, pointing in a new direction.

"Of course not," she muttered mostly to herself. "Why would you. It's not like it would be polite."

And it's not like he cares for me. Just wants to keep the baby safe, it seems.

But she followed him anyway, because what else was she going to do at this point? So off they went, following his new direction.

Uphill.

Great.

CHAPTER 17

Darkness crept in quickly under the tree covered canopy. It was light, and then all at once the forest closed in around them.

By this point Sydney was well and truly exhausted, and in desperate need of a shower. Only the fact that Chief was also looking flustered kept her from being completely miserable. *Even if he's only upset that we haven't made better time, I'm sure.*

The panic that had never really gone away was threatening to bubble to the surface again. She fought it back, but it kept coming, the silence giving her too much time to become lost in her own mind with the demons that lived there. A distraction was necessary.

"Chief."

"Yes?" He didn't look back, keep his attention ahead of them.

"We're going to be staying the night out here, aren't we?"

It was more a rhetorical question than anything. Unless they were close to some sort of civilization, which she doubted, there was nothing but forest for hours in either direction.

"Yes."

She nodded to herself, moving around a slight rock outcropping that Chief had simply stepped over. Damn him and his long legs.

"Where, exactly, are we going to be staying?" she asked. This wasn't preciously the change of subject or distraction she'd hoped for. But at this point, any answer out of Chief was to be considered a win.

"Cave," he answered abruptly, like she should have already known this.

Sydney thought about biting her tongue, then didn't. She didn't deserve this treatment. "You know, it might be obvious to *you*, that that's where we're staying, but it isn't to me. So I'd appreciate it if you'd be a little more polite in answering my questions. Got it?"

"Sorry." It was all the reply she got.

Great. An overnight stay in a cave, on some random mountainside on the west coast of the country. While being chased by bad guys who were after them for some unknown reason. This definitely was the best babymoon ever. Yet another reason not to have had kids.

Not that her desire to remain childless had anything to do with that, she thought to herself, picturing a tiny room under the stairs, and her mother scolding her for not keeping it properly clean.

You should be thankful you get a room. You're too ungrateful.

Nothing but a burden. You need to learn to give back. It'll be for the best.

She shivered as her mother's voice entered her brain. Shrill and unfeeling. As it had always been.

Then there was another sound. A deadbolt rattling as it slid into place, closing her in. A moment later the light would go off, and Sydney would be left alone with her dreams.

And her nightmares.

"Can we stay somewhere other than a cave?" she asked cautiously.

"Need to get somewhere we can keep warm. Cave is the best option."

Sydney didn't bother to hold back her sigh, but she kept climbing, her attention wandering from flashbacks of her youth, to Chief.

He was so calm and unflustered. The entire afternoon and evening as she followed him up the mountainside, not once had he panicked, or lost control of himself. He'd remained calm. Thoughtful. Level-headed.

Almost like he had a plan.

She thought back to the accident, reliving the chase and everything her brain could piece together of the aftermath. Chief telling her to stay relaxed. His quick thinking and instant reactions that had prevented them from being run off the road.

None of this was new to him. That realization shot through Sydney like a lightning bolt, stiffening her spine, and increasing her wariness. Whether this was unexpected or not, he was used to being in perilous situations. Was trained for it.

Who the hell is he?

A slight feeling of relief swept through her, knowing that, if she was forced to be stuck in a situation like this, Chief was a good man to have along. One who could think his way through it and get them out alive. She hoped.

The only problem was that he seemed to have half-anticipated the situation. Sydney took in the hiking pack he was wearing, and all the stuff he'd packed that suddenly helped them out a lot more. All of it to aid them in evading the men after them.

No. They weren't after *her*. They were after him. Chief. Nobody knew or cared about one Sydney Hart, that was for certain. They just wanted Lechiffre, for reasons unknown.

Planting her feet, Sydney came to a halt, hands on her hips. Looking over her shoulder she gazed down the incline, imagining how the mountain sloped away past where the brush obscured her vision. Down to the highway. To civilization.

"Why can't *I* just go back down the mountain, Chief? Back to the highway, and find a ride to the nearest town? Why do I have to hide out in the mountains with you? Nobody is after *me*," she challenged.

Chief had kept walking, and was now a dozen or more steps away. Her voice stopped him, and he turned back, taking in her aggressive stance. Sydney tried to ignore the way his eyes roved across her body with more than a hint of sexual undertone. That was *not* something she wanted to think about just then. Not at all. They were in danger!

"This is my fault," he admitted, crossing the distance to return to her side.

"Uh, just so we're clear, what exactly are you admitting

to being your fault?" she said, not wanting to leave anything cloudy.

Chief winced, and avoided her gaze. That couldn't be good. That couldn't be good at all, in fact. What *else* was he about to tell her?

"You can't go back to the highway because they'll find you and catch you easily," he explained.

"They don't even know who I am," she countered.

"They do now. And they won't hesitate to use that against me."

"What? Use it against you how?" Sydney was confused.

"*Both* of you, against me," he said emphatically, eyes dropping heavily to her stomach. "They'll threaten you, if I don't do what they want." He looked away. "But you have to understand, Sydney, I *can't* do what they'll ask of me. I can't. So my only option is keeping you safe, and out of their arms. Don't you see?"

She shook her head. "No. Not at all. I don't see anything but forest and mountain. I don't understand!"

"I know. I'm sorry about that too," he said, speaking with a gravity that strangely made her believe him this time. That was odd.

"Who is after you Chief? *Why* are they after you? What have you done?"

Chief shook his head. "Nothing, I swear to you. I'm one of the good guys." His eyes narrowed, as if he seemed to pick up on one of her biggest worries. "I am no threat to you, Sydney; of that you can be assured."

She sighed. "Not directly, maybe. But Chief, just being around you has gotten me in danger. Real danger, it seems."

Chief cringed, looking like he wanted nothing more than

to melt away and pretend this whole thing never happened. But he didn't. He straightened. "I know. I'm going to get you out of this, and then, if you still hate me, I'll send you on the most luxurious babymoon you can imagine, all by yourself, without me."

For some strange reason, Sydney found herself disliking the idea. Not the babymoon, that sounded wonderful. No, she didn't like the concept of going without him nearby. That bore some more thinking on.

"Where are we going now?" she asked, changing the subject. There was nothing she could do to change the present. Only hope they escaped long enough to live for the future.

"Deeper into the mountains," he said instantly.

Sydney sighed. "Well that's not ominous. Not in the slightest. Taking me deep into the mountains where nobody else will be."

Chief licked his lips. "You're panicking," he said quietly, as if afraid saying it out loud would set her off.

Her nod was jerky and ragged, brought upon by her impending exhaustion at the hike, and constantly being afraid of what was going on for the past six hours or more. She didn't even know how long they'd been hiking now. It was impossible to tell time, and her cellphone was dead after hours of trying to get signal every two minutes when she pulled it out.

"Yeah, I am panicking," she confirmed. "Don't you think it's just a little bit acceptable and justified?"

"Maybe," Chief said, voice grinding out like rock upon rock. "There will be time for that later. Not now. For now we have to climb. To head upward, where we can find a cave."

The breath Sydney took as he reminded her of where they would be stay was a sharp one. Right. A cave. A tiny space.

"Who gave you permission to come out?"

"I'm sorry, ma'am. I have to use the bathroom."

Lillian Hart rolled her eyes. "You should have held it until morning. I'm very disappointed in you. Go."

Seven year old Sydney had practically raced across the floor and into the washroom under the disdainful eyes of the woman who had brought her into the world. The woman who didn't want her.

"Here," Lillian had said as Sydney came out, shoving a bowl into her hands. "You're interrupting our evening. Use this if you're too weak to hold it next time. I don't want to see you until it's time for you to make breakfast."

"Yes, ma'am." Sydney had taken the bowl and run back to her room under the stairs.

A moment later she heard the deadbolt being put into place. She wouldn't be leaving again if she wanted to.

So she sat in the dark and wondered what she'd done wrong this time.

"Sydney?"

She blinked, Chief's voice cutting through the haze. He was close, now, very close. Right near her. Why was he standing like that?

"Yes?"

"Are you okay? You weren't answering me there." His eyes flicked back and forth between hers worriedly.

Belatedly she realized his hands were wrapped around her shoulders as well. They felt nice there. Warm. Comforting. She almost threw herself into those arms, wishing he would gather her up and tell her this was all some sort of horrid nightmare. A dream she was about to wake up from.

"I'm okay," she assured him, lifting her left hand, resting it on top of his on her shoulder. She let it linger, enjoying the contact. It felt nice.

"Good. We really do need to get going. I can't risk you getting caught out here at night. I need to find somewhere safe for you."

She was touched by his concern for her wellbeing. It was nice to know that, even if the whole cockamamie situation was his fault, he still wanted to ensure she was safe. In a weird, convoluted way, it was sweet of him. She kind of liked being put first.

"I must be insane," she muttered to herself, giving his hand a squeeze and then moving around him, back through the forest in the direction he'd been heading.

"Pardon?" Chief called as he hurried to catch up.

"Nothing," she said sweetly, her voice reeking of false innocence. "Nothing at all."

Yup. Definitely insane. Why else would you still be going with him, and not as fast as you can in the opposite direction? Nobody in their right mind would think that he's actually doing all this to protect you.

She was definitely losing it. Right?

CHAPTER 18

Guilt couldn't begin to describe how Chief felt.

How could it all have gone so poorly?

He trudged along, legs wide, shoulders back, doing his very best to forge a path through the forest that she could follow with ease. It was clear that Sydney was flagging, but still, she had yet to complain. Her strength impressed him, and his respect for her grew with every passing minute.

Quite the opposite, he was sure, of her opinion of him.

Chief had led them into this mess, and he was determined to lead them out, but that didn't change the fact it was all his fault. Nor that he couldn't tell her a thing about what was truly going on.

I could…

But what if she took it poorly? With the way their situation was already dire, doing anything that would drive the wedge even further between them seemed not just inadvisable, but stupid. Telling Sydney could potentially be the catalyst that drove her to go for help, bringing all of the Tyrant-Kings minions down upon them.

Chief would fight till the end, but he doubted his ability to stop them all. He was only one man, in the end, even if he was fighting for the life of his child. Numbers would tell eventually.

No, it was better he kept his mouth shut and kept them moving. If they could just cover enough ground, they would pass into Pacific territory. There, hopefully, he could find them some real safety. Or at least, Sydney could be safe. He wasn't about to dwell on how they might react to his presence.

His own personal safety, however, was the least of his concerns. He would sacrifice whatever it took to get her out of this situation and to somewhere that was *truly* safe. Chief refused to dwell on the fact that the Tyrant-King's men had found him. Somehow.

Could it have been pure coincidence? He doubted it, but stranger things had happened. It didn't really matter at this junction. The only thing that mattered was Sydney and her wellbeing, including that of the tiny being developing within her womb.

Chief didn't want to think of his child. Not yet. It could be a distraction, one that might lead to a mistake. He could afford no mistakes. So he stayed within himself. Quiet. Reserved. *Focused.*

I should have just let her be. She didn't want anything to do with me, and I should have respected that. She would be safe now if I had. Back home, on her farm, working the land like she enjoys. But no, I had to try and play hero.

Look where that had gotten him.

Waiting until the schism within his House was settled, one way or another, would have been the better choice. Chief was well aware that may have meant he wasn't around, if things went south, but it would have kept Sydney out of harm's way.

Like everything, it was all his fault. He couldn't escape that.

"Does it have to be a cave?" Sydney asked from behind as they moved up the mountain.

"Does what have to be a cave?"

"Where we stay tonight."

He frowned. The cave was the best choice. It was easily defensible, well hidden, and most of all, it would be easier for him to keep it warm for her. Chief could sleep anywhere. If he shifted, his wolf would barely even notice the chill that was already entering the air as the sun set.

Sydney, on the other hand, was only staying warm because of their constant physical exertion. He was well aware the moment they slowed, or it got too dark, the sweat would turn cold in a heartbeat, and she would begin to lose heat. He intended to have her somewhere safe by then.

"Cave is the best choice," he said, almost adding *for you*, to the end, catching himself just in time. He didn't want to have to explain that slipup. "We aren't equipped to sleep outside."

Sydney shivered, but he knew it wasn't because she was cold. There was something else going on there. Just like there was something about the idea of her being a mother that she wasn't telling him.

I'm not the only one with secrets I suppose, he realized.

Though hers didn't' seem like the kind that could reach out and kill them. They were personal.

"Are you sure the cave is safe?" she asked, voice quavering slightly even as she fought to keep it even.

"What do you mean? I will make sure it is before you go in." He'd not thought he would have to add that disclaimer. It should be standard, she should know that, but if it helped her realize he was going to protect her, then he would voice it.

"Oh, it's not that," she said weakly. "It's just that I've seen those horror movies. People go into caves, and they explore, then a cave-in happens and they're forced to go deep into the cave to find a way out. But along the way something starts hunting them."

Chief almost chuckled, but he didn't want to be dismissive of her fears.

"Rest assured, that will not happen to us," he said, looking back at her so she could see it in his eyes.

Her face crinkled. "That's what they say in the movies."

Chief chuckled despite the situation. "We're not going cave-diving. I'm talking about a small cave, Sydney. Not a big one."

"But you're sure it has to be a cave?"

"Yes. Trust me, you will be okay with it. It will be more like a...a den," he said.

Sydney lifted her eyebrows, mouth screwing up to one side. "How can you make something so scary sound cozy with just one word? That's not fair."

He chuckled, wishing he could explain to her why the idea of a den was so appealing to him. But suddenly explaining that he was part wolf and could change into one on a whim was probably not the best course of action. Enough mistakes had been made by him already, he wasn't about to make another. No, right now she needed consistency, and no more surprises.

"Perhaps one day I can show you why," he said, fighting back the longing in his voice as he thought of Moonshadow Manor.

That was truly home, not the farm he lived on now. With its winding halls, excessive stonework and snug rooms close to one another, it was just perfect. Until now, he hadn't quite realized just how much he missed it. He would much rather be showing Sydney around the Manor than some random cave on a mountainside. It used to be a safe haven; a place he would have wished to raise the child. Now it was nothing but a memory of pain.

"What do you want to show me?" Sydney asked.

Chief shook his head and motioned for them to move on. "Nothing," he rumbled, dismissing the subject. Reminiscing would have to be set aside for another time. Right now his focus was on Sydney, and getting her to safety.

"I'm confused, what are you talking about?" she said, not letting it drop as they walked on, pushing through underbrush and fallen detritus from the trees above.

"Just gibberish." He didn't elaborate, hoping she would let it drop.

Sydney fell silent, perhaps listening to his unspoken pleas to change the subject. They hiked for another thirty minutes like that, neither one speaking, except when he warned her about a hole hidden by leaves, so that she didn't twist her ankle. They were already moving slow, he couldn't afford any more delays. Not if they were to stay ahead of the Tyrant-King's men.

"Over there." He pointed, guiding them to an opening in the mountainside.

Ducking down at the entrance, he peered inside, senses on red alert. There was a decent chance that another animal had claimed the cave already. Depending on what it was, Chief didn't want to take any risks in evicting it. But he couldn't smell anything but cool, damp stone and dried leaves. If anything had lived there once, it didn't now.

"Chief, that's an awfully small hole," Sydney said nervously as he shrugged off his pack and crawled inside to take a better look.

"That's exactly what we want," he called back softly. "Less heat escapes. Easier to keep warm."

It was also harder to find, and far easier to defend, but he wasn't about to scare her with talk about tactics and such. Sydney was already on edge, and right then he needed to keep her focus off of such things. That was his job. He had to look out for her. Protect her.

No. Not just *had* to look out for her. He *wanted* to, Chief realized. That was a strange feeling, but the more time he spent with her, despite her attempts to keep him at arm's reach, Chief found he enjoyed their banter.

It was fun.

"Warm would be nice," Sydney admitted, finally crouching down so she could peer inside. "Oh, it's bigger inside."

Chief was in a crouch at the center of the cave, perhaps twenty feet back. It opened up into an oblong shape perhaps seven or eight feet in, the ceiling nearly five feet high at its peak. It wasn't enough for him to stand up in, but they could at least sit comfortably.

"It's quite comfy in here," he said, reaching up to touch the solid stone, then went back to the entrance to grab his pack, moving in a crouched over shuffle. "Come on in," he told her, waving her on after him.

"I don't know Chief. It's awfully compact. And dark."

He cursed, forgetting that she couldn't see in the dark like he could. Fishing a flashlight out of the side pocket of his pack he propped it up on some rocks and turned it on, so the beam illuminated the center of the cave.

"There," he pronounced, giving her his biggest smile.

"Right. Um. I'm just gonna stay outside."

She pulled back from the entrance and stood up. Stifling a sigh, Chief went after her, snatching her hand before she could get far.

"What are you doing?" she asked, staring down at the physical connection between them.

"Come here." He tugged gently on her hand, until she was facing him full on. "Down here," he urged.

Sydney closed her eyes. He saw her shoulders rise and fall as she took several deep breaths. Finally she crouched down so they were almost eye to eye. He didn't let go of her hand.

"It's going to be okay," he promised, looking deep into the swirls of her eyes, noting that she had some flecks of orange buried within the brown that he'd never noticed before. Beautiful.

Just like the rest of her.

He ran his eyes over her rounded features, remembering how much he loved the freckles that covered more than just her face. They ran down her neck, over her breasts, stomach, legs. They were everywhere, and he absolutely could not get enough. Each one was unique and different than the rest, and Chief never tired of staring. It was like every time he gazed upon her he noticed something new, because he'd discover a different freckle.

It made Sydney unique in a way he had never experienced with someone before. Might never experience again.

"I need you to trust me," he said softly, squeezing her hand, not tearing his eyes away.

"I don't know, Chief," she started to protest, but fell silent as he reached out and took her other hand, now holding both of them.

"It's okay. I'm not going to hurt you. I promise. I will protect you. But out here you'll freeze, and get sick. In there, I can keep it warm for us. We'll be okay. But I need you to trust in me, and not fight me over it."

Her eyes darted past him to the cave entrance. Chief blinked in surprise as he *felt* a shudder run through her. It came through their connection, where his hand held hers.

"I don't know what you're thinking of," he whispered. "But I promise you, this isn't it. That's in the past. This is different now, Sydney. Trust me."

Her eyes returned to his. They began to search, and Chief realized she was looking for a reasons why she shouldn't trust him. *Or maybe she's trying to find a reason why she* should, *after everything you've done.*

It was true. Chief didn't deserve her trust yet, which would make it all the harder, because he *needed* it. They had to get inside, and he needed to get to work obscuring their trail.

In the end, mother nature decided to help them both out. The leaves of the trees above them began to rattle softly, and moments later the first drops of rain came down. They'd been so busy hiking under the greenery that neither of them had noticed the storm moving in.

"I suppose it's better than being out in the rain," Sydney muttered, closing her eyes yet again as she accepted her fate for the evening. "Okay."

Chief sighed in relief. The first battle was won.

Too bad it was the easiest.

CHAPTER 19

"You know, it's almost like you expected for this to happen," she said as he settled her down into a corner of the cave and pushed an energy bar into her hand. To add emphasis to her point, she brandished the bar in his face.

"I like to plan for all situations," Chief explained. "I told you this. I knew we were taking a less than well-travelled route through the mountains. Better to be safe than sorry, right?"

"Something like that," she agreed, letting enough sarcasm slip into her voice to ensure he knew she didn't' believe him for a second. "Just what else did you pack that you didn't know we would need?"

"Some emergency rations, some heat-reflective tarps, a sleeping pad, rope, duct tape." He shrugged, the motion sending crazy shadows all over the cave wall as he momentarily blocked the flashlight. "The usual."

"The usual," she echoed, tinfoil-like wrapper crinkling as she pulled it open. "Yeah. I don't suppose you have a cell phone battery, or signal amplifier, or flares, or anything we can use to summon help."

"Cell phone battery," Chief muttered, repeating it to himself. "I'm going to have to add that one to the list."

She groaned.

"Look," he said, coming over to sit next to her.

Right next to her. Sydney didn't shuffle away, but she was acutely aware of the pressure against her right leg where his rested against her. And of just how close his face was to hers. She tried to look forward, or up, or to the left, anywhere that wasn't at him, but she kept getting drawn back into the soulful, handsome gaze of his.

That's exactly what got you into this predicament in the first place. Careful.

"We're going to be okay," Chief told her. "I promise you. It's going to be alright."

He was so earnest, so convincing, that Sydney almost believed him. The only thing was, even if he got them out of this jam, there was still the child growing inside of her to handle. It wasn't going to be alright. Her entire life was changed. She was responsible for this little being now. Which was a big mistake the universe had made, in giving it to her, perhaps the one person most unequipped to be a mother. What was she supposed to do now?

Give it up for adoption, remember, you made that decision already.

Right. Giving it away. To a family that could provide better for it. That was what she'd decided to do, because that was the best option for the child.

And for you. Don't act like it's a completely selfless choice.

Well of course it was the best option for her. Sydney

would just screw it up if she kept the child. She didn't know the first thing about how to parent. Nor did she have any role models to draw upon.

Maybe Chief does. He certainly seems eager about the idea of a child.

Yeah, Chief sure was happy about that, though he didn't seem to want anything to do with her. His focus was on the child, and not Sydney, other than that she was the vessel for his unborn offspring. That much he'd made clear by keeping his distance.

You told him to go away.

"How can you know we'll be alright?" she asked, trying to drown out her mind and its conflicting statements. At least it wasn't focused on the cave.

Just as she thought it, her eyes snapped up, to the cave roof just above her head. All she had to do was reach up and touch it. That's how close it was. Tons of rock, just sitting there, ready to fall in and crush them at any time, without warning. This place was a deathtrap, couldn't he see that?

"I know a safe place," Chief was saying. "It's not that far from here. There's a lot of hiking to go to make it there, but we *can* make it on the supplies we have. So you see, we'll be okay."

She stared at him aghast. *More* hiking? Sydney had known logically that they had to hike back, at some point, but now he wanted to take her further into the mountains?

"Does that mean staying in more caves?" she asked nervously, looking around, ever thankful for the flashlight. It was the only thing keeping her fears at bay.

She'd had a flashlight in her room once. It was the only

source of light, but she'd used it sparingly, because little Sydney had known that when the batteries ran out, she wouldn't get any more, not right away at least. So it would be back to the darkness, and the sound of the stairs above her as someone went up or down, the noise like thunder to her child-like senses.

"Maybe," Chief said.

She shuddered at the thought, trying to keep herself together.

"I'll be right there with you," he promised, reaching out, taking her hand.

Warmth flooded her palm, spreading slowly up her arm, combating the slight trembling that hadn't stopped since she'd entered the cave. It took some of the edge off, calming her nerves. It almost made the enclosed space bearable. Almost.

"I don't know if I can do this, Chief," she said, her eyes darting to the exit. "I…"

"Shhh," he said, squeezing her hand, then reaching over to wrap his other palm around her as well.

Her hand disappeared between the two much bigger grips. Latching on to the sturdy sense of protection that Chief seemed to exude at all times, Sydney managed to calm herself ever so slightly, forcing the panic back down. For now.

"Where will we sleep?" she asked. If she could perhaps fall asleep when the light was still on, she could make it through the night. Her body was already shutting down after the hike, so sleep wouldn't be close behind, that was for sure.

"Here," he said, letting go and moving away to the pack, eager to help out.

Sydney looked down at her hand, suddenly missing the sensation of his skin against hers. That simple contact had gone a long way to helping her feel at ease, to push some of the stress aside, giving her something else to focus on, to distract her.

That's all it was though: a pleasant distraction. He was just doing all of this to keep her calm, so that she didn't bolt for freedom out of the cave entrance. It was tempting to do just that, but there was still light from the flashlight, and the idea of the rain wasn't particularly inviting either, though it wasn't coming down hard.

Chief, meanwhile, had spread a silvery tarp on the ground, and was now busy unpacking a sleeping pad from the bottom of his pack, spreading it out on the ground.

"Here," he said, gesturing. "Once you're in, I'll wrap the tarp around you, and add another one. I brought a few heat warms. You know, the little reusable ones you snap and they generate heat? Toss those in there, and in a few minutes you'll be nice and comfortable."

He looked up with a smile. Sydney had to look away before she got lost in his face. It was too easy to look at him for a long time, as she'd learned six weeks ago. He was just that captivating, his strong jaw, ears just a little too big for his face, and then there were the eyes. The twin azure circles were striking, even in the yellowed light inside the cave.

"Where will you sleep?" she asked cautiously, swallowing nervously.

"Outside," he announced. "I'll keep watch. Just in case."

"All night?" she asked uncomfortably, looking out through the narrow entrance.

"Yes." There was a tightness to his voice.

Sydney hated that idea. She didn't want Chief to be outside. Leaving her alone. Locking her in.

It was just like her childhood all over again. Someone pushing her into a confined space, stealing the light, and then leaving. They got all the freedom, while she was forced to stay in the dark. Terrified.

"I promise, I won't bother you while you sleep," Chief assured, misinterpreting her reaction to his words. "I'll leave you in here alone, you don't have to worry."

He smiled, as if he was being extra polite, and turned to go now. To leave.

When he passed closer to her on his way out, she reached out, snatching him by the arm. Instantly the bigger man came to a halt.

"What is it?"

"You don't have to go outside," she said. "There's plenty of room. You know we could make it work. Nobody needs to go outside, or be alone. It's fine. You'll be fine. We can make it work. If I go over there, and you go there, and we—"

Chief leaned in close without warning, lips covering hers.

It burned. Literally burned. After hours of hiking in the cooling afternoon, Sydney hadn't realized just how cold she'd become. When he kissed her, the warm of his mouth was like a thousand needles of agony driven deep into her lips.

She cried out, and in response he kissed her harder,

mistaking it for a sign of agreement. There was no fighting it, and just then, she didn't want to. Sydney needed it, needed the mental slap to calm down the anxiety that had been coming to a boil. This wasn't how she'd expected things to go, but all at once she was transported back to another night, when he'd done much the same thing.

Like then, she melted into him, overcome with awe that this bronze-skinned statue of muscle wanted anything to do with her. She was not the type to attract the muscle-bound hunks, but Chief didn't seem to care.

It was good. *Really good.*

Maybe too good.

CHAPTER 20

Could it all be an act? Was Chief just putting on a show, like guys did in the movies when they were forced to be with someone they didn't want to because of situations outside their control? Was that all this was for Chief, a one-man play where he pretended to be interested in her?

Even actors couldn't kiss her the way Chief was, she thought as he wrapped his hands around her, pulling her in tight, enveloping her not only in his arms, but the aura of heat that seemed to permanently surrounded him. The tingles spread from her lips, across her face, down her neck and slowly out to her extremities. It was unstoppable.

Do I even want to stop it?

What did she want? It was a question Sydney wasn't prepared to answer. Not now, with Chief pressed up against her. Tilting her head back she moaned quietly as his tongue gently flicked out, sliding against hers, warm and soft. Right then, Sydney decided, what she wanted, was to *be* wanted. Wasn't it?

One of Chief's hands stroked her face, and she leaned into it, feeling his fingers push her short hair back, running through it as he moved to cup the back of her head. The temptation to give in was strong. Very strong. Yet the last time she'd done that, she'd wound up with a child—*their child*—inside her.

That means you can't get pregnant again.

With a hiss of indrawn breath Sydney fought down her hormones and their tricky message. She wasn't going to free them, not today. Placing both hands on his chest and pushing, she separated them.

"Is everything okay?" Chief asked, face drawn up in concern.

"Yes, it's fine," she assured him. "I just…"

"You can't."

Nodding, she patted his chest, feeling the firmness of his muscles through his shirt. "I can't," she agreed. "Not tonight, at least. I—"

"Shhh," Chief said, one hand lifting a finger to her mouth. "It's okay. You don't have to justify it, okay?"

This wasn't the reaction she'd expected from him. Sydney had expected he would fight her over it, try to push her to keep going. Instead he was playing the perfect and understanding gentleman.

Was he really playing, though, she wondered? It seemed like he was always trying to be nice to her. Giving her space, or trying to help if he felt she needed it. For a brief moment she felt a pang of guilt, that maybe she'd been judging him in her head still for the whole getting-her-pregnant part.

"Come on," Chief said, grabbing her hand and easing

her across the cave to where he'd laid out the bedroll and reflective blankets on the flattest part of the cave.

"What about you?" she asked as he settled her in. "You aren't seriously going to stay outside, are you? You'll freeze?"

Chief looked down for a moment. "The cold doesn't affect me the same as it does you," he said, looking like he wanted to say even more.

"What does that mean?"

"It means exactly what I said it means," he laughed. "You'll be comfortable in here, and you'll have privacy as well. As much as I can give you, considering," he said, looking away in what she assumed was embarrassment.

Sydney bit her lip, trying to reconcile everything. Her pregnancy, their situation, his desire for her, his seemingly complete and utter respect for her, and if she was being completely honest, also her interest in him.

"Can you get us out of this?" she asked, feeling a chill come over her as a stray breeze worked its way into the cave. She pulled in tighter to herself, trying not to shiver.

"Yes," Chief whispered fiercely, his eyes lighting up despite the dimness of the cave.

She could practically see the cerulean fires burning deep within them. He believed what he was say completely and thoroughly, which went a long way to assuaging her own fears.

"We're not far from a safe place," he continued. "I know it sounds crazy, but you need to trust me, for at least a little bit longer."

"You realize at some point you're going to have to explain everything, right? I'm not going to just accept what happened today and let it slide under the rug. You owe me the truth, Chief, about what I'm caught up in."

"I know," he said solemnly. "I promise to you, I will."

Sydney shook her head. "Why do I keep believing in you and trusting you?" she muttered aloud. "For all I could know, you're some kind of super criminal and those were government agents back there."

Chief snorted. "Absolutely not. I give you my word, I'm one of the good guys. You have nothing to fear from me personally."

"I...I know," she told him, meeting those eyes, looking as deep into them as she could, before she found the barrier, that wall he kept up around his deepest, darkest secrets. Yet even there, that far into his soul, Sydney felt comfortable with him. Like she wasn't a stranger, but in fact welcome.

"You do?" Chief asked, eyebrows rising swiftly in surprise. "I mean, good, that's good."

She chuckled, the sound turning into a shiver as the cool late-night spring air started invading her space. Chief stiffened as he saw it.

"You're getting cold," he rumbled. "Lie down."

Sydney did as she was told. A second later Chief curled up next to her. Then, awkwardly, he shuffled and pulled the two sides of the heat-reflective blanket up and over them. Her shivering was getting worse up until that point. Then, all at once, she felt heat. Real, honest to goodness heat.

"How are you so hot?" she asked as the blankets quickly warmed her, bouncing heat back in against her. "It's nice."

Chief chuckled, the sound vibrating through their connection. "I'm glad you enjoy looking at me."

Sydney sputtered, and started to turn over so that she

could look him in the face, but a firm hand on her shoulder stopped that motion.

"If you do that, I'm not going to be able to resist kissing you," he growled.

She frowned to herself, rolling back to face away. When he'd spoken, Sydney had caught another emotion in his words beyond humor and lust. Had it been...pain? She thought it might be, but that didn't make any sense. Why would it hurt him not to be able to kiss her?

"I'm going to get us out of here," Chief told her, breaking the silence a few minutes later. "Then we're taking a proper vacation. You and I—" He hesitated. "And baby. We're going to go somewhere warm, with sun. A beach. Everything you wanted."

"You're serious about wanting to raise the child, aren't you?" she asked.

"Deadly."

She believed him. Sydney was filled with too many emotions and thoughts to form anything coherent right then. All that she was able to fixate on was the warmth. It was almost like she was on a beach right then. Almost, but not quite.

"Just remember," she said. "No staying over, that's my rule."

"Your rule, eh?" he teased.

"Yup. I have them in place," Sydney agreed, stifling a yawn.

"Why?" Chief spoke softly, almost directly into her ear.

She forced herself not to snuggle deeper into him. Already his arm around her was feeling far too comforting, the contour of his body lined up perfectly to her. It was beyond tempting. Sydney wasn't entirely sure where she was finding the willpower to resist him.

"For good reasons," she said, the yawn escaping anyway.

"And what are those good reasons?" Chief asked.

"So that I don't end up pregnant and sleeping on a cave floor with a man I barely know," she informed him, already feeling sleep rising up, cradling her in its sweet embrace.

"Goodnight," Chief said. "I promise I won't stay over. Now get some sleep."

Sydney was way ahead of him, sleep nearly having sunk in completely.

Don't get too used to this feeling though. You know it will never work out with him, despite how nice it feels to have his arm wrapped around you right now. Don't let your guard down, keep the boundaries up. You know it's for the best.

Wasn't it?

CHAPTER 21

Leaving her side was far harder than Chief had expected, and for much of the night he'd fought the urge to return to her side. Once he'd even found himself hovering over her, watching her face, slack and beautiful as she rested as peacefully as possible given the situation. After a while he'd clued in to just how creepy watching her like that was, and had crept back outside.

That was when he'd busied himself creating a barrier of branches at the cave entrance, which would better keep the heat in the cave, and also stop the wind from getting in. He frowned as another gust swirled through the forest. It wasn't very strong, the slight curve to the hillside and the thick trees doing plenty to help disperse it, but Chief knew if they came to any clearings, it would be quite brisk.

He worried about Sydney. Carrying a child was a lot of work on her system. Even at this early stage, he hated having her do so much work. She should be at home, resting, getting proper nutrition, rest, and care so that she and baby would be strong come birth.

Chief was still determined to convince Sydney that they, or at least he, would raise the child. Foster care was not the answer, and if he could just earn enough of her trust to find out why she was so scared, he knew he could find a way to help her accept that. But earning Sydney's trust wasn't going to be easy.

That's why he'd backed off immediately when she'd wanted him to stop kissing her. Chief was going to need to push, but at her pace, and demonstrate along the way that he could be trusted to behave. That trust would, hopefully, carry over into trust with her secrets. Secrets he could help. Pain he wanted to share.

He frowned and got up from his crouch on the hill above the cave opening, where he'd spent all night watching, just in case anyone, human, shifter, or animal, came to investigate the new scents. The rain the day before would have helped to cover their tracks, but it hadn't been strong enough, not here under the canopy at least, to completely hide it.

During that watch, he'd had a long time to think about Sydney. About him and Sydney. Those thoughts for most of the trip had been focused on her being the mother of his child.

After the kiss they'd shared last night, and his intense, *burning* internal reaction to it, Chief was starting to wonder about the situation. About their relationship with one another, and just where it was actually going. Perhaps he'd been wrong all this time. Perhaps she was more to him than just the mother of his child.

Normally in a situation like this, Chief would go to the Hunter of House Canis. A Title Holder, one of the rulers of the House, the Hunter was blessed with the power to see the strings of fate that connected two mated pairs. While they didn't always appear, it would have most certainly given Chief some of the certainty he lacked right now.

Unfortunately, there was no Hunter among the rebels. Chief was going to have to puzzle this one out on his own, and hope that he didn't make the wrong choice. It was nerve-wracking to go in so blind, without knowing the truth of the matter. How, he wondered, did humans have the strength to do this on the regular? To trust someone with their heart, and not fear that it would be misused?

His ears perked up at the sound of movement from inside the cave. Sydney must be stirring. Though he longed to be able to tell her to go back to sleep, Chief knew that waking her now would be for the best. The light had just started to filter in as the sun rose far to the east, and if they started now, they would hopefully get a good head start on their pursuers.

They hadn't come after them in the night, but Chief wasn't naïve enough to think they were out of danger. Not yet. Trouble would be coming, and in all likelihood, would be on them before they knew it, especially if they stuck around too long.

He couldn't risk his child on giving Sydney a few more hours sleep. Stepping forward, he jumped down to the ground out front of the cave entrance.

"Sydney, it's me," he said before starting to pull away the branches he'd used to cover the entrance. "Time to wake up."

"I'm awake," she said sleepily from deeper inside. "This isn't exactly the Ritz, you know. Sleeping in isn't as enjoyable."

He chuckled, walking in a crouch until he got to her side, where he gazed down upon her face, his eyes picking out plenty of detail even in the limited light. The flashlight was close by, but he'd turned it off after she'd fallen asleep, to conserve the battery.

"Sorry. This place had good reviews on the internet. I figured it would be adequate to your needs. I'll do better next time."

They both laughed, sharing in the light moment, knowing full well it may be their last for a little while.

"Here, I'll pack up, you eat," he said, pointing toward their rations.

"You sure?"

"Positive," he said, shooing her from the bedroll before immediately folding it in swift, confident motions that he hoped didn't come across hurried. The last thing he wanted was to scare her. It was a delicate balance of working to get them moving, yet keep Sydney calm at the same time.

"Are they coming?" she asked, halfway through one of the protein energy bars already.

"I haven't detected anyone," he said. "But they will be, it's just a matter of time. They can move faster than we can. We need to keep our head start if we're going to make it to safety before they catch us."

Sydney nodded and stuffed the rest of the bar into her mouth, then leapt to helping him pack up their meagre belongings into his pack. They took everything, including their garbage. Nothing that could be left behind to trace

145

them, except for their scent. Chief had no way to disguise that, but he wasn't about to make it easier for their pursuers either.

He also didn't tell Sydney that he didn't believe they were going to make it to safety without a fight. The Tyrant-King's men following them weren't stupid. They would note his direction, and they would shift, coming at them in their wolf form if need be to stop the pair from reaching Pacific territory.

A fight was coming. Chief wasn't going to be able to avoid that. So he would have to be wilier than the loyalists. Find some way to get the drop on them, or to throw off pursuit. Something. *Anything*, to keep Sydney and their child safe. That was his primary focus right now.

"You're sure that we're going in the right direction?" she asked as they exited the cave and straightened.

He waited for her to stretch her back for a few moments before setting off in the direction they needed to go to cross the border into Pacific land.

"Yes. This direction. We can make it," he said, hoping against hope he wasn't lying to her face. "But it won't be easy for you, I'm afraid."

"Just walk," she said fiercely. "I'll keep up."

Something burned in his chest as he led them off through the forest, trying to find the easiest trail to take. It was pride, he realized some time later. In Sydney, and her toughness, her unflagging spirit.

What a remarkable woman she was, to display such strength of character despite being so tremendously out of her depth she probably didn't even recognize how bad it was. She wasn't backing down, however, and he had to respect that about her, if nothing else.

So onward they went, deeper into the mountains, Chief leading the way, Sydney clomping along behind him, huffing and puffing, and never once uttering a complaint about the pace he set, or the terrain they were covering. She just *kept going*.

It was impressive, and he wanted to tell her so, but something warned him that drawing attention to it like that wouldn't earn him any points. So he just sent his silent respect flowing toward her.

While at the same time keeping the fear of what would happen once they crossed the border to himself. He'd told Sydney it would be safe once they did, but if he were being completely truthful, he could only vouch for *her* safety. Not his.

That was all that mattered to him though. Getting Sydney to safety, so that she could give birth to their child in time. If his sacrifice was demanded for that to happen?

So be it.

CHAPTER 22

Sydney barely noticed the scenery around her. All she did was follow the path Chief took. Other than that, her mind was lost in its own musings.

Thoughts and memories of the night before flowed through her, mixing in turn with more blurry, heated moments from their first tryst nearly seven weeks ago now at this point. It was that long since she'd become pregnant. It seemed like an eternity.

Without thinking about it her hand went to her stomach. There was no bump there yet, but she knew it was growing inside her daily. Soon she would begin to show. There was so much to do in the meantime as well, planning, preparation. Appointments to be made. It was almost overwhelming to think about doing it all.

Which is why she was distracting herself with more carnal thoughts. Base physical desires and the last time she'd had them sated. By Chief. Their kiss the night before had awoken those memories, and also a renewed surge of want and lust that she'd been fighting off ever since.

It wasn't fair, she argued to herself. How could one simple kiss send her entire body into such a frenzy? Who was he to hold such power over her? Yes, he was gorgeous, and covered in deliciously sculpted muscle that felt like steel to her touch, but was that really all it took to turn her into a pile of lustful desires?

Just the thought of his muscles, and the way his mouth felt on all parts of her body, or how his cock filled her nearly to her breaking point; that was all it took. She cursed her weakness.

"What's that?" Chief asked over his shoulder.

"Nothing," she muttered between breaths. "I'm good. Why, do you need a break?"

Chief coughed, smothering his laughter. "I'm fine," he assured her.

There was an awkward pause to the end of his sentence. Sydney got the impression he wanted to say more.

"Well, spit it out," she told him, easing herself up and over a log.

At the start of their journey she would have hopped over it, but her legs were burning badly by this point, and she wanted to save her strength. Chief was driving them on relentlessly, and though he wasn't constantly looking over his shoulder to see if they were being pursued, she could feel the urgency in every step he took. He was nervous.

"Spit what out?"

"Whatever you were about to say," she huffed as they started up yet another incline.

I hate mountains.

Chief didn't respond. Sydney was about to push, but something about his body-language told her he was still paying attention to the conversation, not ignoring her. Instead she took her time, let him think it over. He would talk when he was ready.

Finally he half-turned, so she could see the troubled look on his face for a moment. "Did you ever, um, you know, consider trying to make it work?"

"Make. What. Work?" she asked, needing a breath for each word. This incline was getting steeper, forcing her to lean forward and really drive her knees.

"Uh. You know. This. Us. Together."

Sydney snorted incredulously. The question was so far out of left field it was the only response she could think of to address the impossibility of it.

"Ah," Chief said, and kept walking. His pace sped up a little.

Hurrying after him, she felt bad. He was hurt by her answer. That set her to wondering. Could he have actually been serious about the question?

"That wasn't a joke, was it?" she asked once they started travelling on level ground again and her breathing grew easier—somewhat.

"No," he said very, *very* quietly.

Hiding the pain. But it was obvious in the way he didn't turn back, and the set of his shoulders, obscured as they were by the pack. Or the stiffness of his movements.

"I…" She paused, taking in several breaths along the way. "You never showed or indicated that you were interested in me in any way," she said.

"You told me not to call after you kicked me out," he

countered. "Just because I respected your wishes doesn't mean I didn't want to see you again. But," he added, interrupting her before she could start, "I was really talking about after you realized you were pregnant."

"Oh." She bit her lip, thinking about it. "No, I didn't. I honestly was furious, and terrified. All of which I mixed into a seething hatred directed at you, because I blamed you for not wearing a condom, and because I was refusing to accept any responsibility for the situation."

"I kinda picked up on that," Chief muttered. "Just a little bit."

"I'm sorry," she told him, realizing with a start she meant it as well. It wasn't just an empty apology. Sydney felt true regret over how she'd handled the situation. "I...I wasn't ready for this, and it scared me. Scares me."

Chief stopped in his tracks so abruptly she nearly ran into him. "I'm scared too," he said, turning around.

"You are?" she asked, shocked.

"Very," he said, licking his lips. "I'm not a father. I've never been one. I'm older, too. I always *wanted* to be one, but it just never seemed to be in the cards. Just because I *want* it, though, doesn't mean I know how, or that I'm not trembling on the inside about screwing it up somehow."

Sydney took that in, mulling it over. "I...what would you want, Chief? A relationship for the sake of the child? Are you assuming that if you stay involved, I'm going to decide not to give it up for adoption?"

Chief didn't immediately respond, he just stared at her.

Buoyed by what she perceived as agreement at her point, Sydney shook her head, realizing how close she'd come to opening up to him. To entertaining the idea.

"That's it, isn't it. You figured that you're worth enough that I'd be overwhelmed and choose you and therefore to keep the child. You just wanted to use me. Is that it then? Am I supposed to be *thankful* that you would be willing to be there? Let me guess, this is guilt from you, feeling like you're forced to offer it up, isn't it?"

Chief was trying to get in a word, but she didn't let him. Sydney didn't want to hear it. Not now. She was tired of the lies and the duplicitous nature of everything to do with Chief. She would be better without him, or any reminder of him, in her life.

"I'm not about to let you change *my* mind," she snapped. "I've made my decision and that's f—"

"Shh," he said, holding up a hand.

Incensed, Sydney batted it aside. "Don't you tell me to *shh* when *iirggh*—" Her words cut off as Chief stepped in close and wrapped a hand around her mouth.

"Be quiet," he hissed. "Now."

Sydney went still as she heard the warning in his voice, saw where his head was looking. Behind them, into the bush.

"We're going to need to run now," he said.

"Okay, I'm— Hey!" she yelped as Chief scooped her up off her feet without asking permission. "I'm not— Chief," she said, knowing her face had to be ashen.

The trees were flashing past as Chief ran, but they weren't what she was focused on. Nor was the incredible speed and endurance he had to possess to move so quickly with her in his arms.

"What is it?" he said, his breath harried.

"Something is behind us."

She could see them, shapes moving in and out of the trees, flowing like shadows as they came on, too indistinct for her eyes to identify. They were far too good at staying hidden for her to see much more than flashes of movement.

Chief didn't reply, but his body seemed to move faster, as if he'd put on an extra burst of speed. It didn't matter. The shapes were coming on, getting closer.

Then all at once one of them burst out from cover, giving her a full two-second look at the shape.

"Oh god," she whispered, holding herself tight to Chief, making his job as easy as possible, even as she looked over his shoulder at what was coming. "Wolves. There are wolves coming after us."

"Yeah," he rumbled, anger filling his strained voice. "I know."

And they ran on.

CHAPTER 23

Chief simply couldn't run any faster. Not in his human form. If he had a moment to shift, and get Sydney on his back, he could move quicker. Not enough to outdistance their pursuers, but he could slow down their rate of gain. Perhaps last long enough to get the two of them into Pacific territory.

They weren't going to give him that time, though. In fact, they were closing so close now, he could hear their paws as they slapped against the forest floor. So far he heard three of them. Just three.

"How many?" he huffed, not trusting his hearing. The noise of the pack bouncing up and down, combined with the roaring in his ears from his heart, and also the terrified noises Sydney made as she clung to him, were all serving to make it harder on him to confirm.

"Three. I think," she said after a moment.

Just three. Not great odds. But not terrible. Chief ran on, trying to formulate a plan in his mind. Something was bothering him about the situation. The wolves were chasing him hard, but so far they hadn't attacked. That wouldn't last, though...would it?

Then understanding dawned. They were operating cautiously, because none of them knew a thing about her. Including whether or not she knew of their kind. So deeply ingrained was the idea of keeping their existence a secret, the Loyalists wouldn't risk attacking him and revealing any sort of clue that hinted they were anything but wild animals.

Really, really, *really* big ones, yes, but that could just be explained as exaggerations stemming from her horror. Chief could explain away his speed and endurance as him being in great shape, combined with adrenaline at the fear of losing Sydney, along with his unborn child. It was flimsy, but it would stick.

Unless the wolves decided to just kill them both. But they couldn't risk that, in the melee, Chief *might* win, or at least drive them off so that she could escape. Which could be disastrous. So for now they chased him on. Eventually he would tire, and the situation would change.

So you'll need to even the odds before then, won't you?

Yes. That's exactly what he would need to do. Chief couldn't run forever. He was going to have to take a stand and fight.

"I'm going to have to put you down," he said, speaking quietly, hoping only Sydney would hear him. "It's going to be abrupt, and unexpected. Possibly even rough. I don't know when, and won't be able to give you warning. I need you to not cry out and give it away. No matter what. Got it?"

"Got it," she whispered.

Chief marveled at her strength. She was somehow, despite everything going on, managing to keep her cool. It never should have come to such a moment, however, and that pissed him off. Royally.

Anger surged through him and Chief latched onto it. Harnessing it. Rage that these assholes were so desperate to kill him, that they would put an innocent woman, and her unborn child, into mortal danger.

His lips peeled back, exposing his teeth, and he ran on like the fury of the wind, waiting for his chance. For the right spot.

All at once he cleared a fallen tree, and they were at the right spot. The ground dipped far lower on the other side, into a little depression.

"Now," he hissed, though he was already moving, crouching low to drop Sydney, arms sliding through the straps of the pack as he slid across the leaf-covered ground, his momentum dying.

Sydney and the pack slid on, ending up in a heap together, with Chief almost at the very center of the little bowl. He reached out and grunted, snapping the trunk of a small tree just as the first wolf sailed over the same fallen tree trunk.

Chief whirled, and before the massive creature hit ground, he connected with his swing. The wolf sailed wide, crashing hard into the ground, and then up and over the lip of the bowl, disappearing out of sight behind it. No time to pause, however, because another wolf would be right behind it.

"Chief!" Sydney shouted in warning, but it was too late.

The other wolf *hadn't* come over the log, but instead around from the side, and it slammed into him, taking him down. Chief rolled, tucked in his legs and then kicked out with all his power into the wolfs underbelly, flinging it free. The wolves were faster than he was, and their claws would rip him to shreds, but the human body had far more agility.

The third wolf, a mottled gray and white beast closed in more carefully. Chief faced it warily. He didn't have time to waste. Already the second attacker was extracting itself from the bushes it had landed in, leaving huge tufts of bone-white fur behind. No sign yet of the first attacker, but Chief knew it wasn't dead.

Something whizzed out of the side and slammed into the flank of the mottled wolf, then hit the ground. Chief almost didn't see the knife, but he knew it could only have come from one person.

Sydney.

He spared a quick glance, and saw her rooting around the pack for anything else she could use as a weapon. Bless her brave soul, but he couldn't let her continue down that path.

The knife, he saw, was still in its sheath. She'd simply flung it as a distraction. Which meant the wolf didn't even realize what it had been hit with. That was his only chance. It would mean escalating the fight, but Chief wasn't sure he had a choice anymore. It was either them, or him, and he wasn't going to risk Sydney's life just to be civil.

Charging forward at the gray and white wolf, he caught the other shifter by surprise. The wolf dove to the side, and Chief scooped up the weapon as he ran onward, not stopping. Out of nowhere, a dark gray wolf pounced through the air he'd just occupied, snapping at him as he went.

The first wolf had rejoined the fight.

Chief dove forward into a roll, knowing what would happen next. Pulling the knife from the sheath as he went he opened his roll early and slashed upward.

The white wolf, aiming to hit him where he would have come out of the roll, howled in pain as the uranium-embedded weapon sliced deep into its belly, spilling blood and guts across the clearing. Its own momentum made the wound worse as it slid across the upthrust blade.

Chief got to his feet and faced the other two wolves. They hesitated. He wanted to call out to them, to tell them to leave, that he would use the weapon on them as well if they came near, but he couldn't. Not with Sydney there. It was too risky.

So instead he advanced upon them, while their dying comrade thrashed and mewled weakly behind him, hoping the pair of beasts would understand his warning: I will stop at nothing to defend us.

The black-furred wolf looked at Sydney, then back at him, and Chief went cold. The two wolves took off as one almost right after, but it didn't matter. That one look had been enough. They knew. They knew about her; about what he was starting to believe was true about her.

She was his mate.

Now they wouldn't hesitate to use that against him when they came back.

And they *would* come back.

"Chief!"

He spun as Sydney came running over to his side. "Are

you okay?" he asked, looking her over, making sure he hadn't hurt her when he dropped her from his arms.

"I'll be fine," she said, waving off his attention. "Maybe a bruise, but I doubt it. You were incredibly gentle. But what about you? We need to get you help!"

"What are you talking about?" he asked, frowning. "I'm fine."

"You're bleeding!" she exclaimed, pointing at him.

Looking down, Chief saw that his legs and stomach were cut in several places. The first tussle with the white wolf, he realized. It must have gotten a few slashes in as they rolled.

Damn. Now he was going to have to try and hide his healing from her.

"It's not serious," he said, pushing away her prying hands. "We need to keep moving. Now."

She stood up, understanding the gravity of the situation. "What's the plan?"

"Safety," he said, looking ahead of them.

I hope.

CHAPTER 24

"You need to put me down," she told him finally, unable to stand it any longer.

"I'm fine."

She glared at Chief and started to slip out of his grip, forcing him to slow his wild dash.

"You are *not* fine," she said as he caved.

"I am too," he protested as she stood on her own feet again.

"Bullshit. Wanna know how?" she challenged.

"How?"

"If you were fine, you wouldn't have put me down just now."

Chief glared right back at her, but he didn't fight her, and that was just another sign to Sydney that he was in worse shape than he was letting on.

"I still don't know how you've been running with me and the pack this fast for this long, but I am *not* going to have you keel over from a heart attack, mister. I don't know the first thing about navigating by stars or sunlight, and dammit, you owe me a vacation in the sun! So we're going to do this properly, got it?"

There was some grumbling under his breath, but no outright protesting.

"That's what I thought," she muttered. "You're exhausted. There hasn't been any sign of pursuit for hours. The wolves have given up by now."

Chief started to say something, but she shook her head. "We killed one of them. They know we're not easy prey anymore. Plus, we've run so far, there is no *way* that the men will find us either. We're safe, okay? Safe. For now. Like, as safe as you can be in the mountains with not much food or anything." She paused in her mini-rant. "Does the place we're going have food?"

"Yes," Chief said, humor on his face.

That was good, she knew. As long as he could still laugh, then the situation wasn't completely dire.

"Okay then. Well, we aren't making it today. You're tired and need to rest. I'm exhausted, we need to eat. So, I assume you want to stay in another cave today?" she asked.

He nodded.

"Fine, how about that one?" she pointed past him to a rock outcropping on their right, where her eyes had just spotted an opening.

Chief wandered toward it, then backed up abruptly and came toward her.

"What's wrong?" she asked.

"Not that one," he said, taking her hand, pulling her quickly along.

Sydney followed. "What's wrong with that one? It looked nice."

"Occupied," he rumbled. "Bear cave. We don't want to be there."

Fear provided a sudden burst of speed and she scooted past Chief. "Come on, slowpoke!" she yelped, suddenly finding the energy to walk for another hour.

She was the one to spot the next cave as well, and after a brief exploration by Chief, he pronounced it empty, and well suited for their needs.

"No bears this time?" she joked as they went about setting up "camp" inside.

This cave was much smaller than the previous one. There was barely room for the two of them to stretch out side by side.

"I can handle that," she said as he tried to take the silver heat-reflective blanket out of her hands. "And that," she added when he went for the bed roll. "I can be of help."

Sydney was tiring of feeling useless. Like a hindrance. It was clear Chief possessed some sort of super stamina, and many times she'd gotten the impression she was holding him back. There wasn't much she could do to change that, but damned if she was going to let him do *all* the work.

"You sure?"

Snorting, she kept working. "You saved me from those wolves. I don't understand how, but you did. The least I can do is unroll some blankets and tarps for you to relax on. I know you're hurting a bit, even if you're doing a decent job of acting like a tough guy and pretending you're fine."

Chief nodded somberly. "Of course, whatever you say."

She finished with the preparations and then went back

and pulled him over, pushing him down. "Rest, you must be exhausted. Between the running and the fight. You need to sleep. I'll stand guard for a bit," she said, placing a hand on his chest and trying to force him into a lying position.

He didn't budge.

"Okay this isn't fair. I'm doing the right thing here. Let me do it," she growled. "I know you're stronger than me. Congratulations. Now lay down and get some rest."

Chief sighed, but did as he was told, lying back on the bedroll.

"Good." Sydney went to head back outside, but a hand around her arm stopped her cold.

"I wasn't taking pity on you."

There was a long pause while she tried to figure out what he was talking about. "With the bedroll?" she asked, confused.

"What? No." Chief waved that off. "I meant earlier. When I asked if you had ever considered us being together. It was a genuine question. One that I meant completely."

Sydney licked her lips, searching for words.

"I'm not looking for an answer right now," Chief said, filling the void. "I'm just telling you so that you know. I'm not faking anything. Just...think about it, okay? That's all I'm asking. Think about it without assuming I'm trying to manipulate you or something. Because I'm not."

It was a fun thought. A pipedream she could let herself entertain in her weaker moments, perhaps. Life with Chief. The two of them. Three, once the baby came. A family. But it wasn't meant to be. Not for her.

"It wouldn't work," she mumbled, looking away.

"What do you mean? Why wouldn't it?" Chief pushed. "There's no reason it wouldn't."

"Because. I'm not good for you."

"What makes you the authority on what's good for me?" he challenged, sitting up straighter.

Sydney kept looking away, staring into the corners of the cave, the exit, the ceiling, anywhere but at his face. "Nothing, but I know myself. I know I'm not a fit for anyone. You can do better."

Chief laughed in her face. It burned, hearing the blunt dismissal of her words. She was so unworthy of him, he wouldn't even believe her when she told him that.

"I respect you, Sydney," he rumbled, his voice taking on that deeper, growly tone that let her know he was getting irritated. "But do not presume to tell me what *I* want. The only person who knows that is me."

She started to protest, but Chief kept speaking right over top of her, voice dropping another octave until it threatened to vibrate the entire cave.

"And right now, the thing I want...is you."

The smart thing to do was to deny him. To say no, to put more space between them. Exit the cave. Anything that would inject some sense of calm into her brain. All she had to do was say *no*. To tell him that it wasn't happening; *they* weren't happening. Chief would respect that, *if* she could get the word out.

He wanted her. Chief had said so himself. That was a dangerous temptation, the idea of being wanted. It burrowed in deep, taking root deep within her core, and tugging ever so gently. A sensual longing that was nearly impossible to ignore.

Nobody wanted Sydney. Not for a long, long time. Now this gorgeous specimen of a man was in a cave on the side of a mountain, his bright blue eyes nearly glowing in the dark. And she was staring back at him, his words having brought her head back around.

How was she supposed to say no to that? To resist someone like Chief. Someone who should have no right in being interested in her, but was, on a level she couldn't fathom. Yet it was right there, in the crinkle at the side of his mouth as he smiled at her, or the depths of his eyes as she stared deep into them, taking his measure as a man.

All of it screamed one thing to her: Truth. Chief wasn't feeding her lies or half-truths. He was here, baring his soul to her, telling her that he was interested in her. Wanted *her*. The only question was, how was she going to respond?

He was unlike any man she'd ever been close to before. Not just his masculine physique, steel-etched muscles and mysterious persona, but also his actions. Everything about him was old-school gentleman, the kind that the media had conditioned her never to expect to find again.

Beneath that, though, was a bit of intrigue. How had he managed to fight off the wolves, or carry her for so long? Some things just didn't quite add up, giving him an air of danger, of secrecy. None of that scared her. It was the commitment, the idea of being *with* someone, that terrified her, because she was so unused to it.

"I don't know, Chief," she said quietly, still timid and unsure, despite the warmth building at her core, desperate to reach out, to take him within it.

"I do," he replied firmly, no trace of hesitation. "Let me show you."

One giant hand came up, stroking her face with the backs of his fingers, every caress sending tingles down her spine. Without thinking, Sydney found herself leaning into his touches, subtly begging him for more. She didn't want him to stop. Not now.

She swayed closer to his seated form, and all at once heat rose up from his body and engulfed her. If she didn't pull back now, it would be too late. Her strength to resist was only so much.

What's the worst that can happen? You're already pregnant.

With a whimper of defeat, Sydney tilted her head upward just in time to meet Chief as his mouth crashed over hers.

CHAPTER 25

The moment their lips locked, one thought made its way to the top of the pile in her tangled brain.

Why did I deny this for so long?

It was so good. Chief was a perfect fit to her. The hardness of his body complemented the softness of hers. His aggression bulled its way past her timidity. His fingers fit every dimple in the back of her head as he pulled her tight.

"This doesn't mean anything," she told him between kisses. "It's just sex."

"Right."

Chief didn't believe her, but with his other hand creeping up the inside of her leg, Sydney flat out didn't care. She'd said what she needed to say, to give herself an out later, once her hormones were sated. Just in case. For now, she could give herself in and enjoy the moment.

With a yelp of surprise, she fell forward, Chief pulling her down on top of him. Her thick waist felt tiny in the grip of his hands, like it was designed to fit there. Chief casually picked her up and deposited her lower, so that she was sitting directly over his groin. Even now she could feel a hard bulge through her pants.

A deep rumble filled the cave when her hips ground gently against him, prompting Sydney to keep moving into him. Watching his eyes roll back slightly into their sockets was most pleasurable to her, as was the growing reminder of what he had between his legs.

Muscles flexed and Chief sat up, arms snaking around her back, lifting her shirt at the same time. Raising her hands, careful not to scrape them over the low-hanging ceiling, Sydney was stripped of her clothes, one piece at a time. Chief set her down on her back to finish the job, until she was completely nude and exposed to him.

She gasped in surprise as he planted himself between her legs, not expecting him to go that far. But he swatted away the gentle push of her hand on his shoulder, ceasing all resistance from her with a long drag of his tongue against her clit. It was slow and gentle, a warmup, nothing more.

It didn't last long, with Chief slowly increasing both pressure and speed until her hips were lifting clear of the floor, brought closer to his eager mouth with a casual flex of his biceps. The easy show of strength and bulge of muscles prompted further arousal, a reminder of just how sexy the man with his mouth between her legs was. And he was licking her, of all people. Her!

"How did I get so lucky?" she whispered, the final word lingering on in a moan.

"I ask myself the same question about you," Chief growled, pausing only barely.

When he resumed, it wasn't just with his tongue. A finger slipped inside her, pulling forth a low cry that filled the tiny cave.

"Don't stop," she begged, breath becoming ragged. "I'm close. So close."

Eyes locked on hers, Chief continued to hold her hips in the air with one hand, while the other curled slightly inside her, finding that soft, intimate spot and stroking it in time with his tongue.

It was too much. Her body couldn't contain it, and all at once she exploded in a rush of wetness that caught both of them by surprise. Chief held tight while she bucked in his arms, beautiful agony wracking her body as her climax reached the crescendo and spread throughout her body.

Chief tried to keep going, but all at once she was too sensitive. "Break," she gasped. "Give me a minute."

He stopped immediately, trying to wipe the sly, cocky grin from his face, and failing miserably. "I'm glad you enjoyed it," he teased, gently setting her hips back down, filling the inside of her legs with tender kisses that served to calm the pulsing of her clit ever so slightly.

"I never said you weren't good in bed." Sydney lay back with a satisfied sigh, her entire body tingling from memory of her orgasm. "Never said that at all."

Chief didn't respond for a moment, though she could hear and feel him moving. Cracking open the corner of an eye, she noted he was now naked as well; thick, long cock hanging hard from between his legs.

"Maybe not," he agreed at last. "But nobody ever tires of a reminder."

"Is that what you're going to give me?" she joked as he spread her legs and lined himself up with her opening.

"That was really bad," he groaned. "Making da— puns, during sex?"

He'd almost caught himself, but Sydney knew what he was about to say. He had been about to call it a dad joke.

Oddly enough, thinking about it that way didn't bother her. Not now. Not in the moment. Especially not when—

Sydney hissed in surprise as an abrupt pressure between her legs reminded her of what was really going on. A moment later, Chief was inside her, his thick cock spreading her wide. She cried out, lying back practically limp as he slid deep in one slow, fluid motion.

"Fuck I forgot how big you were," she bit off, reaching up for his shoulders, digging her fingers in deep, desperate for something, *anything,* to hang on to.

"You okay?" he asked cautiously, leaning over her, resting his thick arms on either side of her head.

Sydney welcomed the intimacy. The cool weather had began to seep past her the barriers of her arousal, but now she was bathed in warmth, wrapping Chief tight and holding his upper body against her as he thrust with his hips alone.

All her fears, the tiny aches and pains of several days of travel, and the tightness of stress faded as they rocked back against one another in the most basic of positions. It wasn't about getting exotic and working their way through a book's worth of ways to do it.

No, it was about each other. The synchronous ebb and flow of one body with the other. The breaking down of barriers and walls. And it was also about feeling really damn good. Chief's cock was great, but he knew how to use it, and that just elevated her pleasure to another level entirely.

"You feel so good," he groaned in her ear before nibbling on her lobe, sending a shiver down her spine.

"So does that," she told him softly, sighing as he continued.

Closing her eyes, Sydney gave herself in entirely, squeezing around his cock, feeling the way his body tightened every time she did.

"If you keep that up," he whispered throatily into her ear, "I'm not going to be able to last for very long. It feels too damn good."

She chuckled. "That's kind of the point."

"You want to stop?" he asked, concerned.

Sydney's chuckle became a laugh, and she wrapped her legs around his waist as best she could, pulling him in even deeper. "Absolutely not. But there *is* a rock under my back that's kinda poking me," she admitted.

Chief stopped, looked at her for a moment, then he too joined in the laughter at the ridiculousness of the situation. "Maybe if you get on top," he said. "You can find a comfortable position."

They rolled and adjusted themselves awkwardly until settled herself over his hips, pushing back with her waist to capture him once more. Loud moans filled the cave. Given complete control, Sydney didn't go slow. She moved fast, alternating between rocking against him and bouncing. Every time she did that, his eyes fastened to her breasts, watching them.

"I'm going to come," he groaned, grasping her tightly by the hips. "Oh shit. Sydney. I'm going to come for you!"

She waited until the last moment, then hopped off, quickly wrapping a hand around the base of his shaft and taking the head into her mouth. Both hands worked his length as he stiffened a second before exploding. Sydney swallowed spurt after spurt as he filled her mouth repeatedly.

Her eyes were fixed on his face, watching it contort with pleasure until he was done, at which point he slumped back against the bedroll and went nearly limp, the only sound a few low groans as she continued to work his still-hard shaft, until he was completely done.

"You didn't have to do that," he rumbled weakly when she sat up and reached for the water bottle.

"I know. But it's practical," she said with a shrug. "We're not exactly in a place where cleaning up is easy."

Chief nodded, the motion slow and unfocused as he relaxed amid his own glow. "Yeah, I wasn't really thinking of that when I booked the place. The website said cozy and intimate, and I guess I fell for it."

Sydney's snort of laughter came dangerously close to expelling more than just water through her nose. Glaring at Chief, she coughed violently for a few seconds to get over it.

"Better now?" he teased.

"Har har," she laughed.

"Come here," he growled, pulling her down to his side, where she could snuggle up to him. They kissed softly several times before exhaustion swept over her, threatening sleep.

"I'm going to take a nap," she murmured as her eyes closed. "Wake me when it's time to go?"

"Sure," Chief said, stroking her hair.

Falling asleep in his arms was a terrible idea. Sydney *knew* that. It indicated she'd done more than just fuck him. Fucking was what she'd meant. To her, that word was crude, it meant for pleasure, without attachment.

By falling asleep with him so close, in his arms technically, she was letting it slip dangerously close to making love. Which implied feelings. Feelings she wasn't going to let herself confess to. Or believe in.

But he was so darn comfortable she just couldn't resist. Plus he was warm...

CHAPTER 26

He awoke with a start. Sunlight was beating down upon the rock at the entrance to the cave, though the angle prevented it from reaching them within the deeper confines. But it was evident that morning had long past.

"Shit," he rumbled, getting up, stretching achy, sore muscles.

Beside him, Sydney stirred. Taking a second to run his hand along her body once, he admired her even through the clothes he'd struggled to put on her half-asleep body. The temperature dictated the necessity of such actions, her health outweighing his desire to see her naked for any longer.

He busied himself cleaning up what little he could, delaying the inevitable for as long as possible, but less than five minutes later Chief found himself waking Sydney from her slumber. She looked so peaceful he wanted to let her sleep, but they'd already slept in.

"It's late," she remarked once she fought off the grogginess of sleep.

"Yeah," he agreed. "I slept in. I must have been more tired than I thought. Usually my body has me up at dawn."

"You did run for ages while carrying me, then fought off the wolves, then ran some more," Sydney pointed out.

"I know. Still, we're late."

There was no point in growing irate over it now. All they could do was get a move on and try to reach Pacific territory before the Tyrant-King's men caught up with them. Before their ill-fated sleep-in, Chief had been fairly positive about the odds of them doing so. Now, however, it was less so.

Looking up at the sky as they exited the cave, he figured it was well past noon. They were going to have to hike well into the night, and hope that Lenard had patrols out on this edge of his territory at frequent enough intervals they would find the two of them were it was too late.

"Do you want me to carry that?" she asked, pointing at the pack he was hoisting onto his shoulders.

"No, but I appreciate you offering. We need to make good speed today. Very good speed."

"Why?" she asked, following him as he set off into the woods, only barely remembering to keep his pace to something she could match. "Hey, slow down."

Chief hauled himself in, slowing his pace. They couldn't afford to move so slow. Sydney was going to have to push herself today, harder than ever before.

"No time to slow down," he said, starting off again. "We need to move."

"For what reason? We have enough rations to last us

until tomorrow. Nobody is out here. We should take our time and make sure we don't do anything stupid," Sydney countered.

"The wolves haven't given up," he said tightly, coming as close as he was willing at this junction to telling her the truth.

"What? How can you tell?" she asked.

"Tracks," was the only answer he was willing to give, once more urging her to pick up the pace.

Sydney seemed to buy that excuse and for an hour or so they travelled quickly, side by side. The brush around them was growing thinner too as they went higher up the mountain before tracking back down on a game trail. It was a risky move, but one they had to make.

The wolves would follow, and once they found the game trail and his scent, they would move along it faster than either of them could manage in human form. But it was the best way to keep their own speed up. The goal wasn't to outrun the wolf shifters forever. It was to make it to Pacific territory before they were caught. Speed was of the essence.

The more the day went on, the harder it became for Chief not to pick her up and carry her, but he had to force the urge down. Conserving his own strength was going to be key. There was going to be another fight before this was over, he was sure, and with the numbers against them, he needed all the strength he could get.

He studied her as they went, through surreptitious glances stolen here and there. Weariness was slowly etching itself into her face, but he didn't care. Tufts of her rust-red hair were plastered to her face, but they were so short it didn't obscure her at all. Normally Chief liked hair long, but the pixie cut looked good on Sydney. She rocked it, and he was loving every minute of it.

As he had loved every inch of her pale, freckle-covered body last night. There was something about her nearly translucent skin, painted with a million brown circles, that gave Sydney a delicate, fragile look, even if she was anything but that. He loved the contrast.

Things were different between them this morning. Chief had "stayed over" the night before, something she'd made sure he didn't do previously. In fact, in the morning, she'd still been tight in his arms, not just next to him.

Chief had meant to get up at some point and let her sleep alone, respecting her wishes until told otherwise, but he'd been tired himself and had passed out before he could. Sydney hadn't said anything about it yet, and he wasn't sure how to take that.

"Thanks for letting me stay over last night," he joked, deciding abruptly that he *was* going to broach that question. If nothing else, it would serve as a distraction from her growing exhaustion with the pace he was forcing her to maintain.

Sydney laughed. "Normally my place doesn't look like that," she apologized.

"Neither does mine," he admitted, only pausing for a second before adding, "Usually it's worse."

There was more laughter.

But Chief wasn't done just yet. "I was wondering. Have you had a chance to consider my question?"

That was what he truly wanted to know. Where did the two of them stand? After the question he'd posed yesterday, and then their unexpected sexual encounter, he wasn't sure if they were tied together or not.

Sydney looked at him sharply, her attention so focused he had to reach out and lift a tree branch before she walked right into it.

"Focus on the path," he urged with a little smile.

"Kind of tough when you bring up subjects like that so abruptly," she said.

"Sorry. I just…"

Sydney interrupted him. "You really mean it, don't you?"

It took him several long steps to truly grasp the emotion behind the question. Sydney wasn't just looking to him for a confirmation, to repeat the answer he'd given her the day before. By her asking him, she was also, for the first time, giving some legitimacy to his claim that he would be there, that he would stick around with both of them if she decided to keep child.

Chief desperately hoped she would. Not just for the child's sake, or his, but for her own as well. Sydney was better than she gave herself credit for, and Chief wanted to show her, but he just didn't know how. Not yet, though he was working on it.

"Yes." It was the only word he spoke in reply. The only one he needed to speak.

"About me. About the child. This is something you're interested in?"

"It's something I want," he corrected.

"I don't understand. How can you be so sure that you want me? The baby is part yours, so that I get. But why me? We barely know each other."

Chief hesitated. Not because he wasn't sure of his

answer, but because he wanted to phrase it properly. Without any ambiguity, doubt or poor word choice. Telling Sydney that he was a wolf shifter would come, and probably soon, but she'd already been traumatized enough on the side of this mountain. That could wait until things were a bit calmer. Which meant using the 'You're my mate' card simply wasn't on the table. Yet.

"You're meant to be mine," he said forcefully. "Our child was meant to come into this world. I know that at the very core of my being, in a way that I cannot explain to you. All I can do is show you, through my actions, that I mean everything I say. I will fight, guard, love, cherish. Whatever it takes to prove this to you, Sydney Hart. Whatever it takes."

She fell silent, deep in thought, judging by the distant look in her eyes. Chief continued to lead the way, hopeful that his words had gotten through to her, that she had taken a measure of him as a man and realized he wasn't lying to her.

But the longer the silence went on, the larger his doubts grew.

CHAPTER 27

They had said very little since then, and Sydney knew it was mostly her fault.

There was nothing she could do about it, though. Her brain was in turmoil as it wrestled with the implications of everything, trying her hardest to come up with an answer to him. An answer that she truly liked and believed in.

Nothing was forthcoming. He occupied her thoughts in an ever-increasing way, and his words had been spoken powerfully, with a ring to them that even she couldn't fault as true. But whatever *he* said, Sydney still had to feel it as well, and the truth of the matter was, she simply didn't know.

It was quick. That was the crux of it all, she thought. Everything was happening quickly. Several days ago her main concern had been with accepting the fact she was pregnant. Then she'd been rock-solid in her decision to give the child up for adoption once it was born. To a set of parents that could raise it properly, in a loving, caring home. Give it the life she knew she could not.

Now everything was confusing and she didn't know what to do. Glancing over at Chief, Sydney came rushing back to reality. It was nearly dark out, and they had slowed to a snail's pace. Chief wasn't willing to let them stop, and she'd long ago stopped complaining. Something was driving him forward, and she didn't know what, but he'd kept her safe at every turn so far. She wasn't about to start doubting him now.

"What is it?" she asked in the soft voice he'd taught her to use in place of a harsh whisper that apparently travelled much further.

Chief pressed a finger to her lips so suddenly she jumped at the unexpected touch. They both came to a halt, practically in an embrace. Her heart was thumping frantically, so loud she knew it had to be audible a mile away. By contrast, when she pressed her head to his chest as they stood together, Sydney thought he seemed as calm as could be.

Then she heard it. A rustle off to her left. Twisting around she stared at the place her ears had heard noise. Then came something else on the other side of her. Too far apart to be the same thing. There was more of them. Sydney stiffened.

"I don't want to die," she said softly.

"I'll keep you safe," Chief said, though they both knew it was an empty promise. He would do his best, she was sure, but in the dark how was he supposed to fight off a pack of wolves that could probably see both of them with relative ease?

"Do you have another knife?"

"What?"

She repeated her question. "I'm not going down without a fight. If they're going to kill me, I'm at least going to take one of them with me. I'm going to give our child the best fighting chance I can."

Chief stiffened at that last, but he nodded, and a moment later pressed the handle of the knife into her palm. "Slice, don't stab," he whispered. "If you stab, the movement will rip it out of your grip before you've done maximum damage."

"Got it." Sydney gripped it tight, then bared her teeth in challenge to the unseen wolves.

"I'm sorry I got us into this," Chief said, putting down the pack and moving to stand back to back with her.

"Shut up. This isn't your fault." By this point Sydney was speaking normally. The wolves knew they were there. Forcing herself to speak quietly seemed like a waste at this point.

"There's a clearing over here," Chief said all at once, snatching up the pack and taking her by the arm. "Come on."

Together they carefully picked their way through the dark until they reached the clearing, just as he'd said.

"How did you know this was here?" she asked as they moved out into the center of it, grass feeling weird underfoot after days of leaves, rocks and twigs.

"Just did," he replied, sounding distracted.

Sydney switched the knife from her right hand to her left, wiping the empty palm on her pants, trying to dry it out. She was terrified. Even with a little moonlight, she could barely see more than outlines of the tops of the trees. Chief, only a foot or two away, was little more than a black spot that moved in her peripheral vision.

"This is ridiculous. I can't see anything. We must have some sort of light source, don't we?" she asked. "In your pack."

"I can see better without," Chief said in that same unfocused tone.

"What? How is that possible?"

"Your night vision will adapt. Trust me."

Sydney wasn't so sure about that. But at the same time, the moon came fully out from behind the cloud that had been hiding it, and the little clearing was bathed in enough light that she could see to its edges now.

"Where are they?" she asked, turning constantly from left to right, scanning the perimeter.

"Don't attack."

She blinked, not sure she'd heard him right. "What?"

Chief grabbed her by the arm. "If you're attacked, defend yourself. But otherwise, don't lash out with the knife, okay?"

"Huh? Why?"

"Because," he said, still staring out at the dark forest. "It might not be quite as it seems. Just trust me, okay?"

Sydney was about to respond demanding that he explain to her what was going on, when the loudest rustle of noise yet snared her attention. Fearing that it was a wolf about to launch an attack, she spun, bringing the knife up to point at the source of the noise.

"What the hell?" she said out loud as a human emerged from the darkness.

She couldn't make out much about them. They were tall, and human. That was about it. The moonlight let her see them moving, but little else.

"Let me do the talking," Chief said tensely.

Beyond confused, Sydney just nodded, relaxing her stance, but not her grip on the knife. Whatever was going on, Chief didn't seemed surprised by it all. Concerned, yes, but not surprised. How was that even possible?

Her brain ran through a hundred different scenarios while the two of them talked among themselves, but eventually she circled back and started with the same ideas a second time. By that point she was growing tired of being excluded. As a grown woman, she didn't need anyone to talk for her, regardless of Chief trying to help.

"Yeah, hi," she said, coming up to the two of them, lowering the knife but not putting it away. "Who the hell are you, and what is going on here? Chief, who is this?"

The newcomer looked down at her, then back up at Chief. "Not here," he said in a gravelly basso that made clear he expected to be followed without question.

"Right here," she countered. "One of you is going to tell me just what's going on. Who are you, where are we, and what the hell am I in the middle of? Because I'm beginning to suspect that there's a whole lot that nobody is telling me. It's time for answers." She turned her head from the newcomer to Chief. "Care to explain, Chief?"

In the distance the howl of a wolf split the silence, sending chills down her spine.

"We must go," the newcomer said in that same tone. "Now. The fastest way we can."

He turned to go, but Chief hesitated. She could sense it,

as much as she saw it.

"It's okay," she told Chief. "You can carry me. I'm not offended. You can move fast. I'm slow. My ego will survive, I promise."

A second howl echoed through the night and she edged closer to where the stranger was paused, as if waiting for them to follow.

"Come on," she urged.

The newcomer shuffled idly. "The girl doesn't know, does she?"

Sydney's head whipped around and then back to Chief. "Know what?" she asked slowly.

"No," Chief replied, speaking not to her, but to the stranger. "I was, um, getting around to that."

The stranger sighed audibly, which only stoked Sydney's anger some more. "Know. What, Chief?" she bit off.

"You are all so short-sighted," the stranger said with another sigh. "That is one of your many faults. I will let you tell her, but we must go. There isn't much time. We are outnumbered, and the only chance we have is to run."

Then he was gone, into the forest, leaving the two of them. A third cry came from much closer. The wolves were nearby, and it wouldn't be long now before they caught them.

"Come on Chief, we need to go. Now."

He didn't respond. Something about his body language told her he was torn with indecision.

"What are you waiting for?" she snapped, grabbing him by the hand and hauling on it hard. "Let's *go!*"

Still he didn't move.

CHAPTER 28

He was backed into a corner.

They had to follow Priam. Only he knew the fastest way to safety in these mountains. There were several other shifters with Priam, but if he said they were outnumbered, that meant the entirety of the team the Tyrant-King had sent after him was nearby. The only chance was to get to Pacific territory. If they didn't, they were screwed.

But he couldn't outrun them on two legs. Not with an entire pack chasing him. The loyalist had numbers, and at this stage Chief doubted they would hesitate about killing members of Lenard's pack if it meant preventing them from allying with the rebels.

You have to do this.

He agonized over the decision for a moment longer, but another howl from nearby told him all he needed to know. The wolves had located them and were closing in. Time was of the essence, and he simply did not have any more to waste dithering over what to do.

"You're about to see some shit," he said in a rough, abrasive voice, trying to get through to her that he was being deadly serious. "If you want me to explain, you're going to have to jump on and hold on for dear life. *If* we escape, I'll tell you everything, I promise. No time for questions now."

The latest howl of hunting wolves was so close he half expected them break through the clearing any moment now.

"What are you talking about?" Sydney yelped, but Chief was already backing away, divesting himself of pack and clothes, forcing his body to adapt.

"I'm sorry, this isn't going to be easy. I didn't want it to go like this."

Then the shift overtook him and he couldn't speak. Even on a normal day the complete and utter readjusting of his body was a painful event. Now, in the mountains, two days without proper food, and already tired and hurting, it was pure agony. White flashed across his vision as his bones reshaped and reknitted themselves.

Thick slate-gray fur sprouted from his neck and then rippled down his torso, all of which was enlarging, growing in size as the shift took place. From the outside it took four or five seconds to complete. But living it felt like an eternity.

His hands exploded in size, fingers curling and thickening, black claws sprouting from his nails. Pain burst from his hips as they realigned themselves, and Chief fell forward onto all fours. The forest around him came into sharp relief as his wolf's eyes took over, enhancing his already sharp eyesight, along with his sense of smell and hearing.

In the distance he picked up the sound of wolves closing

from three directions as they tried a pincer movement designed to catch him and Sydney in the middle.

Chief braced himself a split second before the worst of the change overtook him, and his skull cracked and reshaped itself into a muzzle, jutting forward, sharp teeth hidden carefully, to avoid alarming Sydney.

Another howl broke through his pain, then a very human scream added to the cacophony as Sydney realized what was happening in front of her. The change was complete, and where Chief had once stood, a massive wolf weighing close to five hundred pounds now occupied his spot.

He abruptly sat down, feeling utterly demeaned as he opened his mouth and let his tongue hang out, giving a soft whine. Acting like a dog wasn't something Chief *ever* debased himself to, but there simply was no time to waste. They had a minute, maybe less, before the wolves reached the clearing. They had to *go*.

Which meant convincing Sydney to trust him, and if that meant acting like a dog to get her attention, then so be it. Chief lay down. Then sat back up, then pawed at the ground, huffing, pointing his snout in the direction they had to go.

Sydney was pacing back and forth, alternating between staring into the woods in the direction of the closing howls, and snatching looks of his wolf. "They warned me that pregnancy hormones were something else, but they didn't tell me about this!" she said.

Come on. Get on. We need to go!

His hearing could pick up the sound of paws in the underbrush, growing nearer with every passing second.

Before long he would hear breathing, and the eventual snarls as the Tyrant-King's men reached them, unless Sydney got it together and climbed onto his back.

Pawing at the ground he jerked his head several times in the direction Priam had disappeared into the trees. They had to follow him, didn't she get that?

"You're really Lechiffre?" she asked, looking nervously at his huge fur-covered body.

He nodded, the motion awkward with a neck hinged at the rear of the skull instead of the base, but it served the purpose.

"Crap. That's not possible."

Chief growled and shook himself out, not taking his eyes from her. Sydney still didn't move, frozen by indecision and fear, as she tried to reconcile what she was seeing, with what was coming after her.

Suddenly her head whipped around to the forest.

"The wolves coming after us," she said quietly, as if just coming to a conclusion. "They're like you, aren't they?"

Chief sighed, but nodded again. There was no more time. They were almost here.

"Shit."

Without much more warning, Sydney flung herself at him, leaping up onto the back of his broad back, straddling his shoulders and leaning forward to grab hold of his fur as tight as she could.

That hurts!

There was no time for pain. The nearest wolf was almost on them. Chief's paws tore up the grass of the clearing as he leapt for the far side, following Priam's trail as he disappeared into the woods at the best speed he could manage.

189

Behind him, he heard the other wolves break free of the forest, the sound of their paws changing as they loped across the grass. Hopefully the hiking pack he'd left behind would delay them for a bit, allow the two to gain some ground back.

"This isn't real. This isn't real. This isn't real," Sydney was muttering from his back over and over again as he raced through the brush at a pace he could never have approached on two legs, even completely unencumbered. The four legs simply gave him an advantage he couldn't overcome.

"Where are we going?" she asked as he suddenly zagged to the left, Priam's trail taking an unexpected turn.

How do you expect me to answer that, he asked her mentally, settling on growling, letting her know he'd heard her, and hoping she would understand.

"Right. Sorry. I guess you can't really talk to me. Being that you're a wolf." She giggled, a high-pitched hysterical noise. "Whenever I wake from this, you're going to be in so much trouble. Drugging a pregnant woman, what *were* you thinking?"

He snorted. Audibly.

"What? It's either that, or I have to accept that I really am riding on the back of a wolf as we run through the forest. A wolf, might I add, that is far bigger than it has any right to be. It simply isn't real. I'm tripping. I have to be."

Chief laughed to himself, enjoying the running commentary as he went. Boy was she going to be in for a surprise when it turned out to be real!

The scent was growing stronger in his nostrils, but so were the sounds behind him.

"They're getting closer," Sydney whimpered, tucking herself in even tighter.

Chief's lips curled up in a snarl, though he saved his breath. Unless he missed his guess, he was going to need it all to run. The pursuing wolves must have realized what he had picked up on: they were close to the true border of Pacific territory.

If they couldn't catch Sydney and him now, they risked provoking the wrath of Lenard. Chief doubted that the Tyrant-King would be overly pleased with anyone who inadvertently made his enemies stronger.

Something came streaking out of the shadows, and only a shouted warning from Sydney clued him in to the wolf angling in for the attack. Chief went wide right, and the snarling bone-yellow teeth snatched at his hind leg, only missing by a few inches.

More attacks came, and he was forced to dodge a tightening obstacle course of trees, rocks, bushes and razor-sharp teeth. One of them came close enough that Sydney lashed out with her foot, catching it by surprise as she kicked it in the jaw, sending the attacker tumbling away as it lost its balance.

Each swerve or course-alteration slowed his pace minutely, however, and the pursuers gained ground. He had to make a run for it. That was their only hope, if they were to make it: a straight beeline for safety, hoping he reached it first.

Chief lowered his head and surged forward, putting all his energy into his legs. On his back, Sydney stayed quiet, keeping low, reducing the drag from her body as much as possible.

"You can do it," was all she said, her voice filled with belief.

He ran on like the wind, ignoring the shapes running almost even with him. All he was focused upon was Priam's scent, and the knowledge that they had to be incredibly close. Just a few more feet, he told himself over and over again, repeating the mantra until the words made no sense to him.

Something came at his side. Pain erupted on his left flank. Chief lost his balance.

They tumbled forward, Sydney spilling free from her perch just behind his neck with a shout.

At almost the same time they shot through the edge of the treeline, both of them rolling and bouncing roughly until they came to a halt. Chief shot to his feet and crouched low, protecting his neck as he snarled, waiting for the wolves to finish the job.

But they never came. He could hear them. They hadn't gone anywhere, but not one of them showed their face. Chief was confused, couldn't figure it out. They were toast.

Then Sydney's voice reached him, filled with awe and wonder.

"Chief," she said slowly. "Look."

CHAPTER 29

She stared in silent amazement at the sight before them.

They were at the top of a hill, overlooking a valley tucked away deep within the mountains. Behind them the sun shone brightly, but it wasn't necessary to illuminate what she was seeing. The lights of the village below did that for her.

Soft yellows and oranges rose from lamp posts on street corners, though calling the small pathways streets was perhaps generous. Tiny shops and houses lined the cobblestone laneways, most dimmed, but many still showing signs of life at this hour.

Everything was made from wood, stone, or a combination of both. Smooth flowing arches and round windows gave everything an old-world feel, but she could see several bicycles moving about on the streets, and in the windows there were signs of modern living. It was a beautiful amalgamation of both, and Sydney immediately felt drawn to the place.

"Welcome to our home," the same voice that had spoken to Chief in the clearing said from her side.

Sydney turned to find a tall fellow ripe with muscle standing at her side. He was covered in muscle, and not much else, she realized with a start, averting her eyes.

"Oh, I'm sorry," she said awkwardly. "I, uh, I didn't know. I wasn't looking, I promise."

The man chuckled, and was joined several moments later by a second laugh. One she recognized.

Sydney suddenly remembered the giant wolf she'd been riding on, and looked around for it. But all she could see was Chief. Also naked.

"Listen, boys," she said cautiously. "I don't know what stories you've heard about me, but I promise, they aren't true. We're not doing this."

"Relax," Chief said firmly, walking up to her. "This isn't for you. It's just that clothes don't survive the, uh, change."

"The change," she repeated. "Right. The change. Of course. Why would clothes survive that? That makes no sense. You both definitely lost your clothes from turning into wolves, not in an attempt to both have me."

Chief snarled loudly at the same time the unknown man laughed.

"I do not mean this to be rude, but I am not interested in you that way," the other man said. "Besides, I suspect your man would have more than words with me if I were to try."

"Damn straight," Chief growled protectively, moving up to stand next to her.

Sydney wanted to admire his toughness, but it was kind of hard when out of the corner of her eye she could see his dick bouncing around every time he took a step. It just… killed the seriousness of anything.

"Right. Okay, so just to be clear here, if you don't mind. Both of you are telling me that it's completely normal and natural for you two be able to change into giant wolf creatures?"

They both nodded, though Sydney tried to mostly keep her eyes on Chief. It was easier to ignore one bouncing penis compared to two. Not that there was anything easy about that, especially not when they were so big and— *Enough.*

"And those assholes back there?" she said, pointing at the forest. "What about them?"

"That," Chief said tiredly, "is a long story. One which, unfortunately, is not at an end."

"But why aren't they attacking?" she persisted, confused. "We're all alone here."

"You are under my protection now," the stranger said.

Sydney felt Chief stiffen next to her. "Your protection?" he asked stiffly. "I thought Lenard was in charge?"

"He stepped down some months back. I am Priam, and this is my pack now."

Priam. She finally had a name for naked dude. "Okay. So you're all wolves in disguise. More than meets the eye, which is tough to say, considering…" She looked Chief up and down.

"You must have a lot of questions," Priam said gently.

"I guess. It's like Twilight, except no glittery skin or dark broody people two hundred years old who are unable to get through puberty."

Both Priam and Chief choked back laughs.

195

"I don't really know how to respond to that," Chief admitted once he'd recovered. "Other than to say in real life, the wolves won."

"You're going to explain that comment eventually," she said, wagging a finger at him. "But you can start by answering my questions. Starting with why the hell you waited until a dark field in the middle of the night to turn into a wolf!" she all but shouted, her façade cracking now that they were safe.

"You probably have many other questions," Priam said, stepping closer.

"Like who the heck are you, and where are we, of course. But can you not stand there. This whole naked thing is…a bit much for me."

"You're going to need to get used to it," Priam said, gesturing for them to follow. "It's fairly normal among our family here."

"You brought me to a nudist resort?" she asked Chief as they followed, her eyes fixed either on the buildings beyond, or locked on Chief's eyes. Whatever it took to ignore Priam's firm backside while they walked. He didn't interest her, but Sydney could still appreciate a rigid rear when she saw one.

"Not quite," he rumbled. "And no, I don't know where he's taking us, before you ask."

Sydney fell silent as he preemptively answered her thoughts.

"We have questions of our own," Priam said, raising his voice. "We go to answer them."

"You seem pretty knowledgeable. What questions could you have for us?" she asked.

"Why have you come here? And what new war have you brought to our doorstep?"

Sydney stiffened. "War? What war? What's he talking about Chief?"

Someone approached them from the village, holding something in their hands. It turned out to be sweatpants, a pair for Priam and a pair for Chief. When they were both dressed, the apparent leader of the colony faced them both.

"Come. The Council is meeting. We have much to discuss." Even as he spoke, armed men appeared on either side of them.

There was nothing ominous about that, she told herself. *Nothing at all.*

CHAPTER 30

They followed Priam along one of the larger pathways. It wound back and forth in anything but a straight line, but nevertheless they slowly made their way toward the center of town.

He eyed the guards on either side of them. Their armor was anything but ceremonial, and the swords they wore were worn from use, judging by the hilt. These were men who knew their job, and weren't afraid to do it. If Chief hadn't known better, he would say they were present to protect he and Sydney from any attackers.

Unfortunately, he did know better. *Unlike our intelligence that somehow missed a new Alpha being appointed. How did we not know about that?!*

It irked him. Now they were descending into the heart of Pacific territory, the very middle of their village, and he was going to have to deal with a complete unknown. How was he supposed to convince him to join their cause, when Chief didn't have the slightest clue what made him tick?

The previous Alpha, Lenard, had been a pacifist, but he would stand up in the face of injustice, and fight tyranny amongst his own kind. Chief had expected that a simple laying out of the facts, backed by proof, would be enough to sway him to side against Laurien, the Tyrant-King. Now? Now he had no idea.

So caught up was he in his thoughts, that he nearly missed the unimpressed stare Sydney was giving him as they approached the large stone building at the center of town.

"I'm sorry," he said in response, not sure what else to say. This wasn't at all how he'd imagined things progressing.

"Right. Right. Of course you are."

Chief started to brighten, thinking that perhaps she understood his predicament better than he'd thought. As Sydney continued talking, however, he realized the sarcastic nature of her initial tone, and wisely kept his voice neutral.

"Just so we're clear. What is it that you're sorry for? The part where you can turn into a giant wolf monster, and didn't tell me? Was it that?"

Chief started to respond, but she cut him off, her violent whisper slamming his jaw closed with an audible *click*.

"Or perhaps it was the part where you failed to tell me *other* giant wolf monsters want you, and I presume now me, dead? 'Cause that seems like something you should probably feel sorry for."

He waited, wondering if she was done. She wasn't.

"Maybe I've got it wrong, though," she said thoughtfully. "Was it the part where you had a secret mission that you brought me along to, putting me in danger? To the point I've almost been killed *three* times now. All while trav-elling under a lie? So, which part is it, Chief? Which part are you sorry for?"

"Um. All of it?" he said weakly.

Around him the guards snickered. Chief bared his teeth and scowled at them, but he didn't outright challenge any. He was too tired, not to mention fighting them would prob-ably weaken his position in coming to them.

"Of course it's all of it," she said, dripping sarcasm by this point, along with rolling her eyes. "What *is* your mission? Will you at least tell me that?"

By now they had reached the center of town, and were approaching the stone building that, unless he missed his guess, was at the direct epicenter of everything. It wasn't huge, only two stories tall, and nothing about it was more overly ornate than any other building. The only thing that set it apart was its location.

Basic squared corners and a gently peaked roof marked the outside. Everything was painted a dull gray. Even the double doors at the top of a short stairway were painted gray. The rulers of this place didn't want to draw attention to themselves in any way.

"My mission," he said quietly as they went right to the doors, "is to *politely* ask the Alpha, who I suppose is now Priam, to consider sending aid to our cause." He stressed the word politely for the benefit of the guards. He wasn't here to strongarm anyone. If Priam said no, then they would be on their way. Just like that.

I hope.

"Your cause," Sydney said, seeming to mull the words

over. "Of course. That makes some sense. It doesn't even sound so bad. Depending on what your cause is."

"Everything will become clear soon, I promise," he said. "The deception is over."

"It better be," she hissed, anger at the reminder coming back to the surface. "But it still doesn't explain why you're so nervous. If all you're here is to ask for help, why are you so tense?"

"This fight has already claimed many lives," Chief said heavily. "On both sides. People I used to call brothers, who have been corrupted by the lies of the other side. If we are denied here, then I fear the war will become a longer, more protracted one, that will call many more of my family before it is over." He sighed. "I have seen enough death at this point, but they will not relent. If we're going to win, we need the numbers to take the fight to them."

"I see."

"And," he added in a small voice, "there's the chance that Priam might order us killed for challenging the Pacific's self-imposed neutrality."

Sydney gaped at him.

"But," he rushed on, "if that happens we'll both be dead before we know it, so no sense dwelling on it, right?"

Before she could respond, the doors to the Pacific Council chamber opened, and they were ushered inside.

"Come," Priam said, walking forward into a large circular room. "Let us get to the bottom of all of this."

Chief swallowed nervously, reaching out to take Sydney's hand. At first she was reluctant, and he thought she would deny him it. But as they walked forward, he felt her fingers twitch, and a moment later she sought out his grip as well.

They strode into the Council chamber together. As one.

CHAPTER 31

"Please state your names," Priam said as he settled into the center chair.

Stepping forward, he nodded in greeting to the nine assembled nobles of the Pacific pack.

"I am Lechiffre Canis, ambassador of Logan Canis, former Knight of High House Canis." He stepped back.

Then there was silence.

"You too," he said, leaning over to whisper to Sydney.

"Uh. Right." She took a step forward. "I am Sydney Hart. Um. Companion, to Lechiffre Canis. Unaffiliated with, uh, House High Canis."

There was a whisper at her mispronunciation, but Chief ignored it, giving her hand a squeeze in support as she stepped back to stand next to him, nearly shoulder to shoulder.

Being so close to her was both heaven and hell. He wanted nothing more than to snatch her from her feet and take her to his home. There he could tell her everything, confess his sins and his feelings, and hope that she felt the same. The pull from his wolf was nigh undeniable, and the only thing that stopped him was his duty.

Running away with Sydney was all well and good to dream about, but there was no way for Chief to make it a reality while a war still waged among his people. He needed to find a way to end it now, before it was too late. Only then could he truly explore life with his mate. And his child. First he needed to make the world safe for them.

"So you do not represent High House Canis?" Priam asked as the Council finished talking among themselves.

Chief had to answer carefully here. "House Canis as you know it has been split," he said, deciding that the truth would be the best way forward. No more hiding, no more retreating behind falsities, to try and sugar-coat the situation. Things were bad, and they needed to know it.

"Split?" Priam wanted to know.

"Yes. The King has become a tyrant. He makes decisions detrimental to the House as a whole, and demands obedience, ruling through fear, not respect. Logan, and those of us who have allied with him, believe that Laurien is no longer fit to rule. We fight against the Tyrant King. We wish to move our House forward into the future. Not return it to the violence and chaos of our past."

Priam nodded, the other Council members murmuring softly among themselves, exchanging worried or uncertain looks.

None of it buoyed Chief's confidence that they would be willing to side with him. To send their warriors to help end the Tyrant-King's rule and re-establish order among House Canis. Most of them, he suspected, simply believed that this wasn't their problem. That they could sit this one out, until it was over, like they always did.

Chief suspected that the King would not let that stand for very long if he managed to eliminate the rebels. A group as strong as Priam's pack would be a threat to his rule, even if they didn't have the numbers to win outright. Laurien was far too power-hungry to let them continue to exist outside of his rule.

""So you have come here to ask for our assistance?" Priam asked. "To fight this war."

"To *join* the war," Chief said. "We are already fighting it. Have been fighting it. But too many of those who would join us are neutralized by fear, or already imprisoned—or worse—by this Tyrant-King. They are afraid, rightfully so, that he will kill them. The borders to Moonshadow Manor are closed, patrolled by his most fanatic supporters, who kill any that tried to escape."

There was a hiss of anger, the first real discord he'd seen among the Council. Restricting the ability of a shifter to choose their own destiny was a big no-no among the Pacific. After all, it was that freedom which had allowed them to start their own pack, free from the influence of House Canis, as long as they stayed neutral in all affairs.

A neutrality that Chief was now asking them to break. To abandon their principles to help save the very House that had pushed them out. A House that needed fixing.

"You ask a lot of us," Priam said thoughtfully. "It is likely many would lose their lives."

Chief nodded. "Yes. I won't lie to you. Death has stalked this battlefield before, and will continue to do so in the future. There is little that I can do to prevent that. But all that it takes for evil to prosper, is for good men to sit by and do nothing." He bowed his head. "For too long, those like me and my faction have done just that. We and our fore-bears did just that when Lenard first left the House to found the Pacific. We let him go, instead of standing up and decrying that something was foul in House Canis."

He turned, looking at each of the Council members in turn, meeting their eyes and holding them until they looked away.

"But no more," he said, raising his voice ever so slightly. "No. More. We have found our voice, and the call to action has gone out. Many have responded, many more are trapped, prevented from joining our cause. But not you. You are free. Free to make your own choice on the matter. I cannot force you to join us, and I suspect that my warning that the Tyrant-King will turn his eyes upon you next will fall upon deaf ears."

One or two of the Council members seemed affected by that thought, but most, even Priam, simply stared back at him without flinching. They didn't care, Chief thought. They thought themselves free from such conflict. That their neutrality would protect them.

"I am here to ask you to stand with us," he said. "We have realized the errors of our ways, and I come to you to admit that. Now, help us stop this madman from sitting on the Throne for any longer. Together we can stop him. Together we can bring our entire House back together, *properly*."

Chief wasn't sure his speech would be enough. Nor was he positive that, even if the entirety of the Pacific joined their cause, it would be enough to bring down Laurien and his men. But it would give legitimacy to their cause, and perhaps, just perhaps, spur some of those who were sitting on the fence, to side with them.

"Please," he pleaded. "Help me make this world safe again."

Priam raised a hand, silencing the muffled whispers of his Council. "You speak powerful words, Lechiffre. Powerful words indeed, that speak to us deeply. We will consider them."

Chief inclined his head in thanks. "I—"

His words were lost as the doors behind them slammed open with a tremendous *bang*.

"Will you consider our words as well?" a voice cracked sharply, filling the interior of the Council chambers. "Will you let us tell you the truth of what is going on?"

Chief bared his teeth and pushed Sydney behind him, keeping her safe as he stared down the six shifters that walked inside. The four guards who had escorted them in tensed, hands going to weapons, though none of them drew.

"There will be no fighting on Pacific territory," Priam snapped. "The consequences for that will be death. Do I make myself clear? We are neutral ground. Your war stays outside of our borders. Understood?"

Chief declined his head, bowing low and holding it. "Of course, Alpha."

The head of the Tyrant-King's team, a man named Leighton, bobbed his head. "Clear. We're not here to fight. Simply to tell you the true, unfiltered version of whatever this traitor has filled your ears with."

Chief's growl filled the chamber, but a slender hand

wrapping around his arm reminded him of his true priority in life.

"Don't fight them," Sydney said from behind him, squeezing his arm as hard as she could. "Please. Not here."

Chief was still bristling at the insults from Leighton, but he took a step back, putting more distance between the traitors and himself. He didn't believe them for a second when they said they would respect the no-fighting rule. They were here for their own good, and nobody else's. If they had a chance to kill him, they would take it, without hesitation.

"Find these two a place to stay," Priam said once things had calmed a level. "I will listen to their story now as well."

Chief almost started speaking again, but Sydney tugged violently on his arm. "Come *on*," she growled angrily, yanking again. "Put your ego aside and think. You're just feeding into their plan. Look at them."

Looking at the team, he saw that they were all standing around casually, relaxed and at ease. Comparatively, Chief was across the room nearly straining to get at them. It wasn't the best look, she was right.

"Okay, let's go," he said quietly.

"Thank goodness. I need a shower."

Chief let himself be dragged from the chamber, his eyes never leaving Leighton's the entire time. Though the other shifter was acting calm, the greens of his eyes promised Chief something entirely different.

Death.

CHAPTER 32

"Well, this is certainly the comfiest jail cell I've ever been in," she said, tapping the steel door painted to look wooden.

"It's not a jail cell," Chief replied.

"It's steel disguised as wood. It locks from the outside. There's no windows. Or other ways out. What exactly is it, if not a jail cell?" she countered.

Chief had no response to that.

"Whatever." She pushed off from the door. "At least it's spacious and comfortable."

And it was. Priam certainly wasn't tossing them in an eight by eight box. Their "quarters" had a separate fully-equipped bathroom with shower, as well as a bedroom with sliding doors for privacy. Sydney could see both from the central area, which had a sitting area with TV, desk, and front entry from the hallway outside.

It was comfortable, though the fact it was several stories

underground beneath the Council chambers killed the vibe somewhat.

"Beats a cave on a mountain though, doesn't it?" Chief asked lightly.

She smiled at him, but didn't reply. It wouldn't be fair of her to lash out and tell him she hadn't chosen to stay there, that it was his actions which had left them in that situation.

"Are you going to talk to me at all?" Chief asked after several more minutes of silence.

Sighing, Sydney dropped onto the couch. "What do you want to talk about Chief? Everything seems pretty straightforward."

His hands clenched into fists. She watched him tense, and then relax as he took a deep breath.

"I'm sorry for the deception, Sydney. I didn't expect any of it to go down like this, okay? Everything is happening differently than planned."

"Life kinda does that, Chief. It's why you have backup plans, and also why you usually don't leave the other person completely in the dark. If you'd told me, if I'd *known*, we could have done so much differently. Everything could be different," she added softly.

"I know," he admitted heavily. "I know, and I'm sorry. I see that now. I can't fix it, though. I can't go back and undo everything, even if I wish I could. All I can do is try to straighten things out now, and make it right."

"Make it right," she said, smiling weakly to herself. "Chief, you've put me in mortal danger. Not just me. My child. *Our* child, Chief."

He shuddered, and for a moment Sydney thought he was going to break down. Crying didn't seem his style, but everyone had their own way of managing grief and other strong emotions.

"I know," he said hoarsely. "I screwed up so badly. I..." His knuckles cracked as he flexed again.

"What were you thinking?"

Running a hand over his head, Chief looked up from the floor, blue eyes haunted with the knowledge of what he'd done to her, and their unborn child. "I was thinking that this was the perfect way to keep you safe. We drive out here, I leave you at the hotel, make my plea to their Alpha, wait for a decision. Once it's been made, we continue to the coast. To the beach. I give you the babymoon I told you about. That way you and our child are safe. Away from the fighting. Away from danger. *That's* what I was thinking."

She frowned. "That's actually not a half bad plan."

He shrugged. "Thanks. I thought so. Which is why I did it. But somehow they knew. Somehow they knew where I was going. What route. Where to find me." His eyes snapped up, blue circles glowing bright. "Someone told them."

"What?"

"Someone told them. Back home. It's the only explanation I can think of." Chief frowned. "But why. Why not just disclose the location of our stronghold so they can crush us completely? I don't get it."

"Maybe they just got lucky by finding us the way they did," Sydney suggested. "Weirder things have happened."

"True. That's true." Chief sat in one of the armchairs nearby. "God I screwed this up bad."

She shrugged, trying not to dwell on the fact that she might still be killed, just for coming along. It was there, at the outside of her thoughts, but there was no point dwelling on it. Not now.

"I don't know," she said. "You gave a good speech."

"I did?" He perked up a little.

"Yeah." Sydney flashed him a smile, enjoying the way his face lit up when she did. "Did you mean that? Everything you said about right and wrong, and uniting your House?"

Chief looked at her sharply, as if hurt. "Of course. All of it," he said, straightening.

"Whoa," she said, holding up her hands in peace. "I didn't mean to offend you, Chief."

He shook his head. "Sorry. But why would I lie?"

"Seems to be a running theme this trip?" she suggested.

"I…" He hung his head.

"What?"

"Nothing. Never mind," he said with a wave, resting his forehead in one palm.

"No. Tell me. I'm tired of not knowing."

Chief looked up. "I was going to say that I didn't lie to you. I just didn't tell you everything. But really, that's still purposefully deceiving you, so at what point does it switch? I just couldn't stop myself from speaking fast enough."

"You meant well, Chief. That counts for something, believe it or not. Especially if everything you said is true. If that's the type of person you're fighting. Someone that evil."

"He's worse," Chief told her. "So much worse."

She nodded. "So all those guys, back at the farm. You're all wolf shifters?"

"Yes." He must have noted a look on her face, because

his eyes and forehead narrowed, wrinkling the skin in confusion. "Why, what did you think we were?"

"Uh, a dude ranch?" she said weakly. "Cause like, it's all guys there, and no women, and you're all super buff and... oh god," she said, burying her head in her hands. "I'm sorry!"

"It's fine," Chief said, waving her apology away with the ghost of a smile. "Though I've been meaning to ask. How are you handling that?"

She considered her answer. "I rode on the back of a wolf half the size of a full grown horse, while being chased by half a dozen similar creatures. That same wolf used to be a man I knew. Trust me when I tell you, Chief, *that* is going to take some getting used to. It's not going to be an overnight thing. I'm mostly avoiding thinking about it right now, truthfully."

"That's fair. I won't push you, but I'm open to questions, if you have them. At any time. Don't feel shy."

Nodding, Sydney gathered her thoughts. Chief was a wolf shifter. A werewolf. Whatever. He could shapeshift. That was cool, on the surface, though there was probably a host of problems that came with it. Like how did he even learn about it? How old had he been when—

She sat bolt upright.

"What is it?" Chief asked, moving in a blur to put himself between her and the door. "What's wrong?"

"Chief," she gasped, barely able to force the words out. "Is...is it going to be—?"

"Is what going to be? Is what going to be, Sydney?"

She reached up as he leaned in close and grabbed his collar. "Is there a wolf growing inside me?" she asked in a strangled voice, tilting her head, the room starting to spin. Was she going to give birth to an animal?

Chief started to laugh. Thunderclouds formed across her face as Sydney's anger rose, and the big man quickly smothered his humor.

"No," he said, choking back what she was sure was more laughter. "It's a child. A human child, I promise you that."

"How can you be sure?" she hissed.

"The change doesn't come over us until we hit puberty. We're totally normal before then. Trust me," he said, taking her by the shoulders. "It's okay."

Sydney relaxed, taking several deep breaths in an attempt to calm her system.

"Sorry," she said. "I was freaking out."

He chuckled, staying close. "I understand, and I don't blame you. Having a child is an experience on its own. Thinking that a little wolf might come crawling out of you is just—"

"Stop," she said, shaking her head. "Let's just stop. I don't even want to think about it coming out like you."

The pressure disappeared from her shoulders. "Like me?" Chief echoed.

She'd screwed up. Sydney knew it immediately by the tone of his voice. The pain in them.

"Chief, I—" But it was too late. The damage had been done.

"I'm not some sort of monster," he said quietly, moving back to sit in his chair. "We've been around for fifteen hundred years. We're people, Sydney. Just like you."

"Come on, Chief, I didn't mean it like that," she said weakly, trying to backtrack.

"No?" he growled, eyes flashing with a hint of anger. "Because it certainly sounded like it. But yes, Sydney, to answer your question, it *will* come out like me. Human, but born with shifter DNA. How that will manifest depends on the sex, and also a bit of luck. Which is just another reason we can't put it up for adoption."

"*Now* you're going to bring that back up?" she snapped, her own temper rising to meet his. "Right now, after everything else that has happened, you're going to start that conversation?"

"Yes," Chief shot right back, surprising her by standing his ground without hesitation. "This is reality, Sydney. You can't shake it. You can't deny it. We are having a child, and that child is going to grow up to be a shifter. You have to accept that this is *real*, and start dealing with all that means."

She glared at him, but he just shrugged it right off, not bothering to give her a chance to formulate her own arguments.

"I am *sorry* that it happened the way it did, Syd. I really, truly am. You can choose to believe that, or not believe that. That's your right. But whether or not you can see your way to there being something between us, there *is* a baby growing inside you. Right now. At this instant. We need to work on figuring out how best to provide for that, and to do that, we're going to have to work *together*."

She recoiled at the power in his voice, the strength. His words weren't spoken out of anger. Not these ones. They were blunt, to the point, without sugar-coating anything. It cut through her rising panic at the idea of birthing a wolf-child, something she hadn't been able to just snap her fingers and accept. Everything suddenly came into sharp focus. *Reality* established itself.

I am pregnant. Me. Sydney Hart. I'm going to be a mother. My child is going to grow up to be a wolf shifter. These are the facts.

"This is real," she whispered, repeating it several times over.

Strong arms wrapped around her, and then she was falling into Chief's embrace, his muscles holding her tight as she shuddered. Not with tears or sobs, but with the heavy realization that she could no longer put off acting like everything was fine. It was time she faced the truth head-on, and began thinking about it properly.

Like a parent.

"This is a lot to take in," Chief whispered in her ear, lightly rubbing her back with one hand. "I'm still processing it myself, but I believe in you, Sydney. You have a strength in you that you don't realize. I've seen glimpses of it. But now it's time to let it shine. Let it *shine*, Sydney," he urged.

She shivered and tried to push him away, but he held tight, his strength impossible to overcome.

"Why are you doing this?" she asked weakly. "Why are you pretending to care so much?"

CHAPTER 33

He stiffened, working hard not to let her words crumple him from within.

"Is that what you think?" he asked weakly, caught by surprise, still trying to formulate a better response. "That I've been pretending, all this time? That it's all fake?"

"Come on, Chief," she replied, still wrapped up in his arms, but no longer fighting to get free, at least. "It's classic. You knocked me up, now you feel you need to make an attempt to be with me, for the child's sake. It's so transparent."

Fighting back the instinctive growl, Chief instead shook his head. "I don't think I've done anything to *pretend* to care, Sydney. I've tried my best to treat you with respect, and care."

"I'm not saying you haven't; I just—"

"I'm not finished," he interrupted forcefully.

She fell silent, and he continued, letting the words out.

They came slowly at first, but with ever increasing speed as he talked.

"You wanted a one-night stand when we first met. Some drunken fun, with no chance of it getting awkward in the morning. I respected that, and let you kick me out without even trying to push for more, if you recall. You said no more, I left."

"What did *you* want?" she asked.

"I admit, at first, just something fun. You were attractive, and we hit it off. The sex was great. I would have stayed for another round later that night, and again in the morning, but I wasn't expecting anything at the time."

"See, so we were both on the same page, and—"

He hushed her audibly. "Stop. Replay what I said, *without* your own bias. Listen to my words."

Sydney was quiet in his arms for a moment, then he felt her head shift, looking up at him. Loosening his grip he leaned back so that they could look at one another.

"At the time," she repeated.

"Yes." He nodded. "At the time, that's all I thought about it. I was enjoying a buzz, so were you, I wasn't thinking about much more."

He reached up and brushed the back of his knuckles against her cheek. "Then, however, then you come to me a week ago, and tell me that I'm going to be a father. That you're bearing my child. That was when I started to look at it more."

Sydney shifted. "Look at what more?"

"You. To look at you more, Sydney. Us. To see how we fit together. The way we work well."

She scoffed. "We work well together?"

"We do. Think about it. How many times during this trip have we just done what needed to be done, without having to discuss it first? We just sort of know what the other one plans, and we do it. It's subtle, but when you think back over it, there's not a lot of discussion going on at some points. We just mesh."

"I...guess."

She didn't sound convinced, but that was okay. Chief had been spending much of his time lately thinking about what he'd just told her. It had taken him some time to even come to that conclusion himself, because of how seamlessly they often operated. Sydney would need some time to think back on it, to see what he saw now that her eyes were open.

"We would work much better together as well," he said, deciding to push a little. "If I could just figure out how to get you to trust me. To tell me what's bothering you so much about this whole situation."

"You mean, aside from finding out that you can transform into a giant wolf?" she said bitterly.

"Yes, aside from that," he said gently, gripping her chin and tilting it upward. "I'm talking about the fear that you disguise with sarcasm and denial."

Her throat pulsed as she swallowed in what he assumed was nervous anticipation. Chief thought about stopping, about letting it stop there, but he couldn't. Not now, not when they were so close to their end goal. He had to ask, to try and penetrate her defenses.

"Why?" he whispered.

"Huh?" She frowned slightly, chin still in his light grip.

"Why are you so adamant on giving up this child, Sydney?" He licked his lips, and plunged ahead with the real question that had been on his mind. "Why do you hate kids so much?"

CHAPTER 34

Trying to control the violent tremor that ripped down her spine was nearly impossible. It practically tore her chin from Chief's hand, and her body convulsed visibly as his words hit home.

"Sydney?" Chief asked, his voice full of concern, as were his eyes.

Shaking her head, she ignored him, trying to maintain control. To keep her composure, even while her hands began to shake and the world grew blurry as tears filled her eyes, and quickly spilled down her cheek, leaving warm tracks behind, but not for long. More tears fell, nearly nonstop.

"I don't hate kids," she whispered through the haze, thankful that she wasn't a sobbing, snotty mess. Tears she could handle, could work through, even if they were accompanied by a sharp stabbing pain in her chest, courtesy of many memories running through her head.

"You don't?" Chief asked, surprised. "I...okay."

"I don't," she repeated. "Really, I don't. Secretly, I've always loved kids. Their innocence, and wide-eyed wonder for the world at large is something that has always filled my heart, Chief. You can't help but marvel at them, wishing they would stay that way forever."

"It truly is a wonderful thing," he agreed, one hand reaching up to wipe away her tears, though more continued to fall without delay. "But if you don't hate kids, then what is it?"

More memories bubbled to the surface. Memories of her own parents, and the way they had treated her. A horrible example of parenting.

"I can't," she whispered, voice so hoarse it cracked. "I'm sorry Chief, I just can't."

"Please don't shut me out," Chief said, pulling her tight into his arms once more, holding her against his chest.

He was so strong, and compassionate. Always willing to do whatever it took for her it seemed. Chief would make a good father, she knew. He understood.

"You can tell me, Sydney. What is it? Are you afraid? Don't be. You would make a wonderful mother."

She stiffened at his words. "No I wouldn't," she said, rejecting them. "I wouldn't make a wonderful mother. Not even a good mother. Don't stay that. You don't *know* me, Chief." She tried to push away from him, to separate them.

For the second time in as many minutes though, Chief held on, his strength easily overpowering her. "I'm not letting you go," he said fiercely. "I'm not going to abandon you like that, just because you want to run away. No more. *Tell me.*"

Shaking her head, she shuddered as the first sob came forth, her control failing her.

"You're wrong, Chief," she said, needing several breaths to get the words out. "You're wrong."

Instead of relinquishing his grip, Chief only held tighter, stroking the back of her head, forcing her to use his shirt to soak up her tears.

"How can you know that, Sydney? You're not even willing to try. I can see things in you that you either can't, or refuse to believe are real. I see a strength in you that laughs at the challenges life throws you. All you need to do is let it free. To *embrace* it. You can't tell me you're not right for this job. You can't know that."

"Yes I can."

Chief growled. "How can you know you would be a bad mother?"

"Because!" she shouted. "Because I don't know how! I don't know what to do."

Her head bounced slightly as Chief chuckled at her outburst. "Nobody does, Sydney. It's a learning process the whole way."

"That's not what I mean," she whispered. "I don't know how to be a mom. I never *had* one."

"What do you mean?" Chief asked, confused. "Everyone has a mom."

"No," she hissed, sitting up straight, forcing herself free from his cocoon. "Everyone has a *mother*. There was a woman who birthed me. She was *not* my mom."

Chief looked at her without speaking, but it was obvious he was beyond confused. "You're going to have to explain that a bit more please."

"My *parents*," she spat the word, "were anything but. I was, I would assume, an accident. Which is precisely how they treated me. Like I was unwanted. Not just unwanted, but a hindrance. I had ruined their lives."

She recounted to him her bedroom under the stairs, where she had stayed until she ran away at seventeen to live with a friend. How she wasn't allowed out, forced to sit there in the dark for hours on end. The constant dismissive attitudes and sighs any time she needed anything.

"Sydney," Chief said, his voice raw, pain rampant on his features. "I'm so sorry you had to grow up with that. Nobody should be made to feel like you're unwanted."

"Well I did," she stated. "That was my example of a mother. It was the only one I ever had. Never anything to do with being a mom. A friend. Someone who cared. Not me. I refuse to do that to someone else. To a child who doesn't deserve it."

"So don't," Chief said.

She shivered. "I don't know what else to do."

"Care for it. Love it. Give it the attention that you wished you had. The help, advice and care that you would have wanted growing up. Don't let that biological womb of a parent dictate how you act. Life doesn't work that way Sydney. You can *be* more than her. You can be *better* than her."

"Can I though? I wouldn't know what to do. I *don't* know what to do. How do I even care for it while pregnant? What do I do?"

Chief smiled, taking her hand in his. "We'll figure it out together," he said earnestly. "If you'll let me. We'll find you some doctors, we'll read all the books. Attend meetings and classes and god forbid, the social media groups full of crazies. We'll do it all. *Both* of us."

"I don't know, Chief," she said. It sounded awfully tempting, to have someone there with her throughout, to keep her from going off the rails. Almost like it was too good to be true.

"You're going to be a far better mother, and a very good mom," he said emphatically, giving her hand a squeeze at the same time. "I know it."

She sighed. "How can you know that though?"

"Two reasons," he said promptly. "One, I can see it in you, right now, in the emotion you're displaying. You're better than she was already, and you're already going to get better. You *want* to be, even if this is unplanned. Because you care. You have a heart."

She smiled weakly. "Thank you. And the second?"

"The second." Chief burst into a grin. "The second is that I intend to be there the entire way, and you can bet your sweet ass I'm going to give you an earful if you start acting out of line. Not that I expect that will happen. You have a good head on your shoulders."

Despite everything, all the emotion inside her, turbulent and unrestrained as it was, Sydney couldn't help but laugh. It surprised her, to be able to see the humor in something so serious, but there was no denying it. She felt better because of it.

The other thing she couldn't deny, was that Chief really, truly did seem to believe everything that he was saying. About her, the child, them. All of it. His words rang with a truth that she doubted could be faked. Still…she needed confirmation.

"You believe all this, don't you?" she asked, placing her other hand on top of his, stacking their hands high as they rested on her knee.

"Yes," Chief said with a fierce hiss. "I do, and I would really like for you to start trusting me that I'm not lying about it. Nor am I deceiving you, or holding back any truths."

"I'm sorry," she said, tears running anew.

This time they spilled because of happiness. Sydney still had no idea what she was going to do after the birth, but for now she could rest easy knowing that she wouldn't have to take this journey alone. Chief would be there with her every step of the way. By her side, helping her, supporting her, leading the way. Whatever it took, she *believed* him when he said he was going to be there.

"Don't be sorry," he chuckled, reaching up to brush away the tears. "Not now at least. But feel free to say it often once the hormones start."

She laughed as he winked at her.

"Come here," he said, leaning in and pulling her face to his, covering her still lightly trembling mouth with his.

Sydney squeaked in surprise, but quickly relented as Chief pushed her down onto the couch, his strength pushing back the last of her fears, in a wave of relief that was swiftly heating up into something more.

Something better.

CHAPTER 35

"What if they have us on camera?" she whispered between kisses, unable to control her hands from pulling him down harder on top of her.

Chief paused mid-kiss, the cutest little thoughtful look frozen on his face. "Good point," he rumbled, before brightening. "Shower?"

"Outta my way," she teased, making like she was going to push him off. "I like the sounds of that."

One powerful arm slid under her and suddenly she was airborne, clinging to his body with her arms and legs while being carried to the shower.

"This works too," she giggled, kissing his neck and earlobe sensually, enjoying the increasing volume of his growls as she did.

Somehow he managed to get the water running with only one hand. Jessica was ready to slip off from him and undress, but Chief had other plans. He pulled open the glass shower door.

"Hey, wait a minute, I— Eeep!" she yelped as water poured down from the ceiling, warm and luxurious even as it soaked their clothing.

"Is there a problem?" he asked, pressing her up against the tiled wall, kissing her through the falling water.

"Yeah," she gasped, the contrast of the cool tile to his burning skin amplifying her arousal. "Wet clothes come off much harder."

Chief grabbed the front of her shirt, but she stopped him. "This is all the clothing I have, mister. You will not rip it."

He paused, then reluctantly lowered her to her feet so that he could strip her. He was slow and careful, which lent the movements an intimate air as piece by piece he exposed her body to his eyes and mouth, both of which devoured her hungrily, before ignoring the torrent of water that splashed across his face as he sank to his knees between her legs.

Hissing in delight, she lay back against the tiled wall, the warm water pleasing to the touch, though it was nothing compared to the furnace burning between her legs.

"You are so good at that," she moaned.

Whether it was her words, or the reaction of her body, something spurred Chief, and in a fit of primal desire he grabbed her ass and calmly lifted her from the ground. Crying out in surprise, Sydney suddenly found herself in the air, back pressed to the tiles with Chief's tongue still playing across her clit. It was *hot*. She'd never been treated so casually before, manhandled without a second thought while he pleasured her, and a fresh torrent of wetness flooded her, only to be lapped up by his eager tongue.

It didn't take long for her body to grow tense, stiffening slightly with every lick as Chief brought her to the peak, and then pushed her over, his grip tightening as she writhed in the air, suspended by the wall and his sheer strength. Pleasure reached out and blasted her senses, overwhelming them for long moments.

Unlike before, this time Chief didn't stop. He picked up speed while also lightening his touch. Sydney was shaking, by this point, voice stripped from her, the only sound emerging from her a wordless moan that filled the shower, as the pressure between her legs built rapidly to another orgasm.

Her hips bucked hard against his face as she exploded for a second time in as many minutes. Chief's grip tightened, holding her against the wall with ease despite the involuntary thrashing as her body ploughed through a second climax. It faded faster than the first, leaving her exhausted but floating on a cloud of satisfaction.

"I need to sit," she gasped, pushing his face away. "Give me a moment."

Wordlessly Chief lowered her to the ground, ensuring she safely collapsed into a puddle, water lapping against her sides.

Her eyes found him, treated to a show as he stripped his own wet clothing off, revealing his taut stomach and beautiful toned upper body to her eyes. This was a sight she would always appreciate. How could you not, after all? He was *gorgeous*, and for some crazy reason, he wanted her. Her, of all the people he could have.

"Why me?" she asked suddenly.

"Huh?" Chief paused, his pants halfway down his legs.

"What is it about me?" Sydney knew it could ruin the moment, but she *had* to know. "You know, that makes you attracted to me."

"Look at you," he growled, finishing undressing. "You're perfect. So lush and wonderful. Your body is a complement to who you are, and it radiates a strength that I find intoxicating, if you must know. Every moment I find myself fighting to restrain myself, not to touch you, to take you."

She shivered at the heat of his words, the fervor with which he spoke. He wasn't lying, she could tell.

"You could have anyone, though," she countered. "Humbleness aside, you must realize you're, well, gorgeous. Any girl would throw themselves at you."

To her surprise Chief *blushed*. Then he sat down on the shower floor next to her, water pouring off his head. He had to blink rapidly, but he kept his perfect blue eyes on her the entire time.

"Yes," he said bluntly. "I know women, and many men, in fact, consider me attractive, and would easily come to my bed. They want me." He shrugged. "But I want you, and that's the difference."

Now it was Sydney's turn to blush, and it only grew worse as Chief spread her legs, revealing her to him completely. She was still gently pulsing from his earlier attentions, but that didn't matter. She wanted him inside her. *Now.*

Chief understood, his eyes focusing on her lustfully, ranging across her body as he lined up with her entrance, rubbing the tip against her playfully. Before she could even admonish him to stop and just *fuck* her, he was already pushing inside.

One long motion later, she was trying to dig her fingers as deep into his back as he was inside her.

"Holy fuck," she moaned, throwing her head back with abandon as his cock filled her, stretching her walls with that delicious mixture of pain and pleasure that she'd come to look forward to with him.

It bounced off the shower floor painfully. "Ow," she whimpered, reaching up to rub the tender spot.

Chief beat her to it, cradling her head gently.

"Do I need to stand you up and bend you over so you don't do that anymore?" he teased suggestively, all the while rocking his hips against her, getting her used to his size.

"I want to look at you," she told him, pulling his face down to hers, kissing him through the water that continued to fall across both of them.

Chief stayed hunched over, his face inches from hers, while moving his hips. Her eyes rolled back as he withdrew and pushed deep, repeating the motion over and over, his focus nowhere but on her.

She couldn't stop it. Another climax built and ripped forth from between her legs in the span of seconds, forged by the intimacy of the moment, the locked eye contact, and the movement of his perfect cock.

Chief lay still as she went limp under him, chest heaving from the repeated hammering of her system. Her body simply wasn't used to this much pleasure. Nobody had touched her or pleased her the way he did. Ever. It was all so novel and new, and yet overwhelming at the same time.

"You can stand me up now," she whispered in his ear. "I'm ready for you. I don't think I can take anymore," she laughed.

"We can stop then," Chief told her, sitting back slightly, though still deep inside her.

"Oh, I can take more of *that*," she said pointedly, running a hand along his abs. "I'm just not going to come again, is what I meant. It's your turn. I want you to fuck me until you do."

"Are you sure?" he asked with cautious eagerness.

"Oh yeah. I'll stop you if I need it. Got it? Otherwise, I'm yours, Chief. Take me."

With a deep, lusty growl Chief withdrew and helped Sydney to her feet, bracing her against the wall. He killed the shower, the water working against her natural lubrication. She felt him step close, and with a hiss she took him deep inside her, shivering slightly as his hands wrapped around her waist from behind.

He started slow, pulling nearly all the way back, before thrusting against her, keeping a firm grip on her hips. Sydney whimpered and moaned, practically melting into the wall. It felt so *good*, and hearing him grunt and groan as he fucked her was beyond arousing as well.

"Harder," she heard herself beg.

Her ass exploded in pain as he slapped it hard, the sting only adding to the pleasure he was inflicting upon the rest of her.

"Fuck me harder, Chief!" she ordered, thrusting back into him, capturing as much of his cock as she could.

He slapped her other cheek in time with a hard thrust,

his speed building, matching the increasing volume of her cries and his groans.

Then all at once he roared loudly, the sound starting out as her name but becoming wordless as he went into what she could only describe as overdrive, thrusting as fast as possible. Sydney had thought she was done. Had known she didn't have another in her.

But the instant he erupted inside her, the explosion of heat triggered a response and she clamped down around him, her legs shuddering as she fought to stay upright. The rest of her body was practically limp, only the wall and his hands on her hips keeping her upright as ecstasy blasted away the last of her strength, blanking her mind while Chief filled her from behind.

"I need to sit down," she all but whimpered as Chief slowed.

"Yeah," he gasped. "Good idea."

The two of them slumped to the ground. At the last moment Chief pulled on her hips, dumping her into his lap. She yelped at the direction change, but immediately snuggled up into his embrace, both of them fighting for air, their hearts laboring to circulate blood.

"That was…" Chief trailed off, unable to complete his sentence.

"Yeah," she agreed. "It was."

"It's gonna take me a bit to do that again," he informed her.

"I need a shower and a nap before we do that again. Sorry to you," she said, reaching between them to stroke his still semi-hard cock with extremely gentle touches.

Chief shuddered, eyes rolling back into his skull. "I think I'll survive. But it might take some drastic measures."

Sydney grinned. "Oh yeah? Like what?"

"How do you feel about being little spoon? In the bed?"

She whistled. "My. You don't half-ass things, do you?"

Chief twisted so he was looking at her dead on. "I'm prepared to have your whole ass, if that helps."

While Sydney choked on air to come up with a response to the double-entendre, Chief reached up and turned the shower back on, dumping warm water all over her head.

CHAPTER 36

He awoke from his slumber feeling refreshed and invigo-
rated to a degree that had Chief re-examining just how tired
he was from their flight through the forest. Of course, it
didn't hurt that he'd spent the night with Sydney.

No, not just Sydney. She's more than that to you. You know
that now, don't you? You've seen it. Felt it. She evokes so much
more than arousal.

It was true. He could no longer deny the theory that had
been bouncing around in his mind. This was his mate. She
was right there, fast asleep in the bed next to him. Reaching
out he run his fingers along her arm, not hiding the smile
that crossed his face as she shifted slightly, pushing back
toward him, seeking out his warmth, his touch.

He wanted to wake her, to tell her the wondrous news.

But he didn't. She was sleeping too peacefully for him to
disturb her. Besides, enough had already been thrown on
Sydney's plate. If it came up naturally somehow, he would
confess it to her, but for the moment, Chief was content to

wait until she'd adjusted to all the other world-shattering news she'd received in the past few weeks.

Pregnancy. Shifters. Etc. All of that would take her time to not just accept as real, but become *comfortable*.

His stomach rumbled and Chief slipped from bed, finding spare sweatpants and shirts in the dresser drawers. Some things, it seemed, didn't change, though the Pacific had opted for black, instead of the more traditional gray that House Canis used.

Food. Where was he going to find food. It hadn't been a high priority the night before. Now however, his appetite was back in full force, and so too, he suspected, would be hers. Padding over to the door he tried the handle.

To his surprise, it was unlocked. Curious, he pulled it open all the way. The hallway outside was empty. The pair of guards that had escorted them there were gone. There was no way it was an accident, which meant Priam must have decided not to keep them locked up.

Chief looked back at the door to the bedroom where the sleeping Sydney still lay. He wanted to tell her, to leave a note, but their phones were dead, and there was no pen or paper either.

"Guess I'll just have to hurry back with food."

Decision made, he slipped out into the hallway and retraced the steps from their journey down, which soon led him back to the surface. He passed several wolf shifters along the way, but besides a friendly nod of the head, none of them said anything.

Apparently their status as prisoners had been formally retracted.

Now if he could just find somewhere to *eat*, Chief would

officially be able to say that things were looking up. For now, his stomach was controlling his mood, and it was beyond hungry, and starting to dive into the realm of hangry.

After finally finding the exit, he emerged onto one of the laneways that served as streets in the village. To his surprise, there were many more shifters wandering around than he'd expected. The numbers of the Pacific were larger than anyone back at House Canis had estimated. A lot higher.

Most of them looked at him, giving friendly nods, though their gazes did linger. Chief was one of the few wearing sweats, he realized. Most of them were dressed in normal clothing, meaning he did a good job of standing out.

"You look lost."

He turned to see Priam come wondering up to him, a gentle smile on his face.

"I only have the layout of my quarters memorized," he returned.

"Ah. Yes. Sorry about that last night. That was as much for your protection as ours," the leader of the pack said by way of apology. "I had to get the others sorted, and listen to their argument as well, without worrying that somehow you or they would find ways to strike at one another. The enmity between your sides is obvious."

Chief nodded stiffly. "Regretfully yes, it is."

"You are free to roam now, however, so please, take advantage of it. Enjoy our home. Those loyal to the King have been quartered on the outskirts of our village, to the north," Priam said, pointing. "They too have been given free rein to wander and explore. But note that if you start anything, you *will* be brought to pay. There will be peace, Lechiffre. Understood?"

"Of course," he said, standing up straight. "I would never dare to insult you like that. I will do my best to ensure I avoid them entirely."

"That would probably be for the best," Priam said with a nod.

"Yes. And I'll get started now. Where can I find food? Something I can take back for Sydney and I to share."

The Alpha grinned, and gestured to the east, where the sun was rising high over the mountains now. "Eamon's is the best. Quickest way there is two blocks down, hang a right after the hardware store. I would join you, but alas, I am meeting with the Council again to discuss everything."

Chief nodded and bid farewell to the Alpha, declining to say anything about the situation. Priam knew the stakes, he knew the sides. The man was a good Alpha, as far as Chief could tell, and so he didn't bother to put pressure on him. It wouldn't do any good. The man was in charge, and he would make the decision that he felt was best for his people. That was worth respecting.

"Eamon's," he mumbled under his breath, following the directions, heading down the side street two blocks, like Priam had said.

An alley opened up on his right and he took it, wandering between the stone buildings. Up ahead it merged with another street, where he could see people once again walking. There were certainly many more than the fifty or sixty shifters present that he had expected. If Chief had to guess, he'd put it at closer to two hundred, an astonishing figure that—

The fist came out of nowhere, lashing up from below and to the side as the shifter came up from hiding behind an outcropping on one of the buildings. Chief reeled to the side, vision spinning as he slammed into the stone exterior hard, wincing at the pain in his shoulder.

Something kicked out his knee from behind and it collapsed, unable to support his weight. Instead of falling straight down, Chief flung himself forward into a roll, getting back to his feet, legs spread, arms up, ready to engage whoever had hit him.

Two shifters in black blocked the alley back the way he had come, evil grins on their faces. Chief didn't know their names, but he recognized the faces as men who had come with Leighton. Loyalists to the Tyrant-King.

"So much for respecting Priam's order not to fight," he spat, squaring up against the two.

"We're not fighting," the first one on the left said, his square face twisting into a sneer. "Fighting means even. This is a beatdown."

"I can take you two pussies," Chief growled.

The second one snickered. "Two?"

Something slammed hard into the back of his head and Chief went down hard, bouncing off the cobblestone ground. Ringing filled his ears and he tasted the metallic tang of blood as it filled his mouth.

Someone growled and hands grabbed his arms and legs, half-lifting half-dragging him in to the nearest building as another figure held open the door.

Chief had been hit hard before. Having his bell rung was nothing new, but the double-impact on the cobblestone had left him dazed, his limbs not properly responding. Before he could get his wits about him, he was tied up and immobilized with enough rope even his prodigious strength wouldn't be able to break it.

"Did you get the guard too?" a voice asked a moment later.

"Yup. He came around the corner expecting nothing. Now he's having a little sleep in a doorway, courtesy of our friend here. Or at least, that's what they'll think." A gloved hand ripped part of Chief's shirt free. "Just gotta go leave this behind."

"That righteous prick Priam will never side with him now. Not if he thinks Chief here knocked out one of his guards and then disappeared. Too much distrust. He'll remain neutral, and then we can crush him at our own leisure."

Enough of the fog had cleared for Chief to recognize the voice as belonging to Leighton, leader of the Tyrant-King's men. The asshole was trying to frame him, so that Priam wouldn't choose his side.

That was the least of his worries, though. He didn't care about that; about the war. All Chief cared about was Sydney. His mate, and their baby. Without him, they were unprotected. Unguarded in a world she was only just beginning to understand existed. They needed him. Needed Chief.

And he was trapped here, in some random building. He had to get free, and get back to them. Before it was too late.

CHAPTER 37

Rolling over, she reached out for Chief, seeking his warmth. The covers had fallen to her waist at some point and she was chilly. He would cuddle her up and bring her heat.

When her hand encountered empty bed, Sydney made an unhappy sound. "Come back to bed," she called sleepily. "Chief?"

He didn't respond, forcing her to finally open her eyes, and accept that she was now awake. That didn't make her happy, and she pulled up the sheets with a *harrumph*.

"Chief, where are you?" she called, raising her voice so that he would hear her from the other room. "You there?"

There was still no response. Frustrated and cold, she sat up. It was then she noted that one of the drawers to the dresser in the bedroom was open, and Chief's old clothes were on the ground.

Now that she was clean, the idea of putting dirty clothes back on wasn't overly appealing. Clean clothes would be wonderful, though the odds of them having anything in her size was unlikely. But upon further inspection, after summoning the courage to leave the warmth of the bed behind, she found the top drawer fitted with a large array of sizes.

"Oh and socks too. How wonderful."

Feeling more refreshed than she had in several days, Sydney did a quick examination of the rest of the rooms to ensure that Chief wasn't hiding on her. It quickly became evident that he wasn't there. She was alone.

Oddly enough, her first thought was that she missed having him around. Not worry, or curiosity as to where he'd gone, but wistful remorse that he wasn't nearby. She wanted to steal some of his warmth, and a hug. Maybe a kiss. Or just enjoy the deep rumble of his voice as he talked to her about nothing.

You're falling for him.

"No shit."

It hadn't really been a question of whether she *was* or wasn't. Sydney was smart enough to know better. The debate she'd had—and was still wrestling with somewhat— was whether the person she was falling for was real, and whether letting herself do so was a good idea.

There was no clear answer to that, but then again, emotions were rarely clear. Especially when it came to caring for someone, opening your heart to them and letting someone get close enough that they could hurt you. *That* was anything but clear. It was often murky, and terrifying, like a horror movie.

But if it was true...

Sydney had been in love before, but not often. She mostly kept to herself. It was just easier that way. Chief, however, wasn't giving her that option. He was bulling his way into her life, and the only way she would get him out was to firmly, and unequivocally, say *no*. Something she just wasn't prepared to do. Not yet at least.

It was truly bizarre. Their trip had gone from dull to disaster in a heartbeat, and from then on it had been nothing but a terror-filled trip through the mountains that she barely remembered. Yet despite all that, she found herself wanting to spend *more* time with Chief. To have him closer to her.

"Which is tough, since he's not here."

Her stomach rumbled loudly and she brightened. Maybe he had decided to go for food. Now wouldn't *that* be wonderful. Adorable, really. After all, she thought, glancing at the clock, it's already nearly lunch time. I need *food*.

Twenty minutes later, however, he still wasn't back, and she was starting to get impatient. Had Priam come and taken him for some sort of meeting? Why hadn't he woken her and said so, or left a note?

Irritated, she went over to the locked door and yanked on it.

"Ack!" she yelped, stumbling backward in surprise as the door opened smoothly, throwing her off balance.

When she recovered, she noticed that the hallway wasn't empty outside. Two heads were poking through the door, looking at her.

"Everything okay?" one of them asked.

"Just fine. Little bit of miscommunication between me and the door. Nothing serious really. Um, what are you doing here?"

The one guard shrugged. "Priam sent us here. With

Chief out and about, he wanted to ensure you were protected."

Well, that settled that argument. Chief *had* left.

"Are they together? How long ago did Chief leave?" she asked. "Take me to them."

The head on the left spoke again. "They aren't together. Priam mentioned something about him getting food."

"That was some time ago, however," the second said thoughtfully. "He must have gotten distracted."

"There's a surprise," she muttered, straightening up. "Alright, well, let's go find him, shall we? This place is bigger than he made it seem, but it can't be *that* hard to track down an outsider, right?"

The first head chuckled. "No, no it shouldn't. If you're ready, we'll take you to some of the more likely places."

"As long as they're still serving food," she announced in time with yet another rumble from her stomach. "I am *starving!*"

The pair of guards exchanged smiles, guiding her up through the building and out into the streets of the little village that the Pacific called home.

"This is a nice place you have here," she remarked as they wandered along some of the laneways. There wasn't a car in sight, and while there were people moving about, it certainly wasn't busy. Everyone smiled at one another, and it didn't take long for Sydney to feel almost at home among the residents.

"We're a close community," one of the guards told her. "Not a lot of trouble. Everyone who comes here does so for a reason, and that helps us create a harmony you won't see many other places."

"You certainly don't," she agreed, following them up a pair of stairs into a little store that smelled of all kinds of delicious breakfast food. "I don't have any money," she realized suddenly. Anything like that would have been in the pack, which they'd abandoned in the meadow the night before.

"Not to worry," a voice said, bustling out from the back with a tray of fresh-baked sweets unrecognizable to Sydney's eyes, though her nose screamed at her to stuff one down. "I heard about your journey here. It's on the house."

Sydney frowned at the elderly woman. "I can't take your charity," she said, "but I appreciate it. I'm really just looking for Chief. Uh, the man I arrived here with," she added at a blank stare.

"Oh, yes, I heard about him as well. Haven't seen him. Have you tried Eamon's?" she asked, using tongs to carefully take the circular cookie-like sweets from the baking tray and move them to a display case. "He's the other breakfast place here."

"Not yet," one of the guards volunteered. "We're heading there next."

"Good. Good." The shopkeeper took up the last one and held it out over the counter. "Here. Take it, before I drop it on the floor and waste it. That's an order."

"Thank you," Sydney said, embarrassed, moving to take it as she was told. "I appreciate that."

"Of course, of course. We look out for one another around here. Can't have a young thing like you going hungry."

She flushed at being called young. It wasn't a comment

she heard often anymore in her mid-thirties, but it was appreciated. Taking a bite of the cookie her eyes went wide.

"Dis if so gud!" she exclaimed around the mouthful of crispy dough, warm honey and something else. Cinnamon maybe? She couldn't tell. "It's heavenly!"

"Glad you like it. Now go find your man," the woman said, shooing her off. "Go, go on."

Sydney was out of the store and down another street before realizing she hadn't protested about the woman calling Chief "her" man. They were...well what *were* they, she wondered. Something, there was no denying that, but they hadn't exactly discussed it last night.

How did she feel about the idea of Chief being her man? Moreso, how did she feel about being Chief's? He was kind, caring, thoughtful, wanted the world for her. Could there be something between them? More than just lust? Maybe. Maybe there already was, and she'd been ignoring it, denying its existence. Had she?

The thoughts swirled around in her head, leaving Sydney more confused than anything. She didn't have the answers to a question the old shopkeeper hadn't even asked. How was it that a silly assumption that the two of them were together was prompting such self-retroflection in her?

"We're here, ma'am."

Saved from the confusing morass of thoughts and emotions currently swimming inside her, Sydney looked up to see they were stopped outside a similarly little shop with the hand-painted wooden sign above it that read *Eamon's*.

"So we are," she agreed, pulling open the door and

heading inside, quickly wolfing down the last of the cookie she'd forgotten she was holding.

"Hi, how can I help you?" a friendly voice boomed out from the far wall.

Sydney stopped, unable to speak because her mouth was full of said cookie. Great timing. She forced herself to swallow quickly so she could answer.

"Hi, um, I was wondering if you'd seen someone."

"Who?" The large man turned around from the counter he'd been bent over, his eyes landing on her. "Ah, you are the new girl. If you're asking if I've seen anyone unknown this morning, the answer, I'm afraid, is no. Not until you."

"That's weird," Sydney said. "Where else would someone go for breakfast here?"

"Sally's?"

"We came from there," one of the guards spoke up.

"That's not like Chief," Sydney said. "The man loves his food. He wouldn't go anywhere without eating—unless…"

"Unless what?" the other guard asked.

"Let's go find Priam. Maybe he went to have another conversation."

"Impossible." Guard number one was shaking his head.

"What? Why?"

"Priam has been in a meeting with the council all morning. It is closed door."

Sydney thought for a moment. "Take me to see him. Something is wrong. Chief isn't anywhere to be found. Nobody has seen him, he hasn't gone for any food, and he's not at the quarters. He's either with Priam, or something has happened to him."

"They're in a closed meeting," Guard number one said stiffly.

"Do you want to be responsible for whatever has happened to Chief, or for interrupting a meeting?" she challenged. "Take. Me. To Priam."

The two guards looked at one another uneasily, neither willing to take the responsibility of what they were about to do.

"Now!" she snapped.

"Better do as she says, lads," the large man, whom she figured had to be Eamon, rumbled from behind the counter. "Something smells fishy. This place isn't big enough to get lost, not this early in the morning. Something may have happened to that poor boy."

Confronted with one of their own agreeing, the guards caved and led her back to the meeting chamber at the center of town. As soon as they were inside and Sydney recognized the route to the main chamber, she pushed past the guards and flung the door open herself.

Priam and the Council were seated around an oval table that hadn't been present the day before, with various papers spread out between them.

"Where is he?" she asked, not slowing down even as two more guards came to block her path. "Where's my man?"

"You mean Chief?" Priam asked cautiously, looking at her with a mix of curiosity, respect, and irritation at being interrupted.

"Uh, yes. Where is Chief? Nobody has seen him today," she said, trying to hide the frown at her initial choice of words.

"I saw him this morning," Priam countered. "Out for a walk. He was hungry. I sent him to Eamon's. You should go ask him."

"I just did," Sydney said hotly. "He hasn't seen anyone new. And before you say it, we went to Sally's first. Nothing. He's not at the quarters either. What have you done with him?"

Priam stood. "We haven't done anything," he rumbled. "And I would ask you to have proof before you level such accusations."

"Well he didn't just up and run away," she fired back, not willing to cave so easily. This was Chief. He would have torn this village apart to find her, with his bare hands if need be. Sydney didn't have the strength to do that herself, but she wasn't about to be dismissed out of hand. Something was wrong, and they were going to get to the bottom of it.

Sydney planted her feet and refused to be moved, staring down Priam, challenging him to do something. Anything. She wasn't leaving him. There was no *way* she was raising this child on her own.

Wait. What?!

"Gather some men," Priam barked suddenly, coming to his decision, providing a most welcome distraction from her internal thoughts.

Sydney nodded once. *We're coming, Chief. Just hold on.*

CHAPTER 38

"There are two options," Priam said, coming over to her, leaving the rest of the Council behind. "Assuming he did not, in fact, just run off."

Automatically, Sydney brought one hand to her stomach. "He wouldn't," she said quietly.

Priam's green eyes flicked down, widening slightly in realization, then he nodded once, the movement sharper, crisper than anything so far. He too shared that same instinctual protection of offspring that Chief had. Was it a shifter thing maybe?

"Adams, I want ten men here, on the double. Plain clothes. Do it *quietly*. Make sure they're all trustworthy," he added, looking at one of the guards.

"What are our options?" she asked, ignoring the pained tone with which Priam had spoken the last in. It was clear the community wasn't maybe quite as united as they made it out to be.

"First, you should know that there is a faction here, one

that would see us even further removed from House Canis and all that goes on there. They would see us go from a neutral stance to one of enforced isolationist. No contact, no relations. Nothing. Any who came here other than to seek shelter and join our cause, would be…dealt with."

Sydney recoiled in horror. "You think they got ahold of him?"

"I don't know." Priam shrugged. "They're a very minor faction. We think."

"You think?" she exclaimed, terror beginning to build at Chief's wellbeing. "That doesn't sound very positive."

"We don't know," Priam told her. "They're very quiet. Their true numbers are almost impossible to tell. This would be the first time they've ever done more than simply argue their case." He paused. "But it's also the first time something like this has happened here."

Sydney took a deep breath, forcing herself to remain composed. "Okay. And the second option? Leighton?"

"May be," Priam agreed heavily. "I told him to stay away, not to cause trouble. But I don't see who else it could be."

"That's who I'm afraid it is too," she said quietly. "Chief mentioned to me that he feared they didn't care about angering you or your pack. That they had a mission and would do whatever it took to complete it."

Priam glanced over his shoulder at the rest of the Council, who were talking quietly. "Some of us got that impression too, but we've long survived out here by *not* getting involved in the politics of House Canis. Some think that is the best way to go from here. Others realize that maybe they're growing tired of us out here defying them."

"So it's Leighton and his men then. We're agreed on that."

"We have no proof, Sydney. Besides, it would be most bold of them to act against my commands, while in our territory." His green eyes glowed with jade fire.

"Why is that?"

"Because I would kill them for such insolence," he snarled. "And that, the Council would back me up on."

The doors to the Council chambers opened, admitting a group of men. Though they were dressed like civilians, she eyed the hard eyes and quiet, alert attention exuding from each of them. There was no doubt that they were all soldiers. Men who would be up to the task of taking on Leighton and his team, if it came to it.

And it will.

Sydney was positive it was them. They had been near ruthless in hunting her and Chief down on the mountain. Why stop now, when their goal was within reach? Knowing Chief, he'd let his guard down, trusting that everyone would obey Priam's orders not to fight. It would have been easy.

"Where do we go now?" she asked as Priam prepared to address his men.

"To talk to Leighton," Priam said heavily, but without hesitation. "My gut tells me he's behind it, and I do not want to waste time. Chief is under my protection, and I will not see my word sullied by those pricks."

The Alpha snapped his fingers and the men filed out of the chamber. They knew what was going on, there was no need for a speech. Sydney and Priam followed behind. She stayed close to the Alpha, well aware she was out of her depth here as a human, and yet never once considering not going. This was Chief.

This was *her* man they were going after, and she was going to be there when they found him. No matter what.

The "crowds" parted as they walked along the main laneway, the dozen or so members of the community quickly clearing a path as they came, and then closing in behind them.

"I'm sorry you have to do this," she said to Priam as they went. "It must not be easy for you, or your pack."

"We chose neutrality. It has worked well for us in the decades we have been here. But everyone knows that others out there may not respect our decision," Priam said heavily. "That we may eventually have to fight to defend it. If Leighton *is* behind this, then it will also weigh heavily on the Council's decision."

Sydney glanced up at the Alpha of the Pacific. "You don't agree with it," she said suddenly, picking up on a note of disdain in his voice.

"I would prefer to remain neutral," Priam agreed. "And I will continue to argue that, no matter the outcome. But whether we join the fight or not, *this* is something I will not let stand."

She nodded, falling silent as the buildings grew farther apart. They had reached the outskirts of the tiny little village. Priam pointed to a fenced off area, where three smaller buildings were grouped together to form a slightly larger compound.

"There."

The guards fanned out, forming a loose arc with Priam and Sydney at the center.

"Adams," Priam said, summoning one of them. "Stay here with her. Protect her."

Sydney wanted to protest, but she knew that it would be of no use. If there was fighting to be had, she was a liability, nothing more. Plus, she needed to start thinking of more than just herself. She would be endangering her child if she went in there. No, better to set her ego aside, and let Priam and his men do the fighting.

Falling back to the edge of the nearest building, the two of them watched as Priam walked up to the encampment and shouted Leighton's name. She frowned, wishing he hadn't given the asshole the time of day, and had instead just stormed the property. But some things had to be done a certain way, she supposed, and this was one of them.

"It will be okay," the guard, Adams, said quietly from behind her. He'd stopped watching and was now leaning idly against the building.

Sydney, on the other hand, was glued to the scene unfolding in front of them. Nobody was answering Priam. Nor could she see any movement inside.

"It's like the place is empty," she said. "Nobody coming out, nothing. Either that or they're inside just ignoring Priam for some reason. What do you think, Adams?"

Out front, Priam and his men advanced, heading into the compound.

"Adams? They're going in now."

There was a *thud* from behind her, and then the sound of a limp body sliding down the side of the wooden building. Sydney spun just in time to see Adams fall into a pile and stop moving. She wanted to scream, but a hand appeared over her mouth, and another pressed a knife to her throat as she was hauled back around the building bodily.

"Not a peep, or you die here and now," Leighton hissed into her ear. "Got it?"

She started to nod, but the knife dug into the skin at her throat painfully. Leighton got the hint, however, and tossed her to one of his lackeys.

"Move it," he said far too calmly for someone who had just violated the orders of an Alpha on his own territory. "Let's get out of here. The plan is working beautifully. By the time they realize what's up, we'll be long gone."

All around her, the rest of Leighton's team chuckled evilly.

CHAPTER 39

He could hear Priam outside, shouting for Leighton.

They were so close. He tried to call back, but the gag in his mouth muffled most of the noise before it ever got out. Angrily, desperately, he heaved against his bonds once more, but Leighton had been thorough. Normally, rope wasn't enough to hold a shifter. But enough of it, at proper strength, would do the job. If they'd just bound his wrists he could have gotten the leverage to snap the fibers and escape.

Unfortunately, Leighton wasn't an amateur, and he'd wrapped paracord from the middle of Chief's hands up to his shoulder, before adding some sort of harness around his elbows, to further decrease his mobility. He wasn't going anywhere, not after they'd done the same to his legs.

The door crumpled under a blow and flew inward, narrowly missing his face. Four guards rushed in, with Priam right behind them. Chief thrashed and worked to get free, trying to convey the urgency of the situation. If Priam was here, that meant Sydney was unguarded. He needed to get to her.

The guards came over, one of them producing a knife. He quickly cut Chief free, the big shifter standing before the job was complete, heading for the door. His legs, bound uncomfortably for several hours, were numb, and he stumbled and fell as blood rushed back to them in a series of agonizing jabs, like a thousand needles rupturing his skin at once.

"Chief. Relax. It's okay."

"It's not okay," he said hoarsely through chapped lips, his mouth dry from the gag. "Not at all. Where's Sydney?"

"She's fine. Outside, with one of my best guards. Really, it's okay!" Priam tried to tell him.

"No, she's not!" Chief shouted as he pushed himself to his feet, forcing down the pain with a snarl that filled the room, bristling with anger at the way he'd been played.

"What do you mean it's not?"

"Where do you think Leighton and his men are!" He went for the door, one step at a time, his legs screaming in protest, but obeying nonetheless. Chief was on a mission. He was unstoppable, a little pain wasn't about to slow him down. "They know, Priam."

"Know what? What are you talking about?" Priam arrived at his side, supporting him, though Chief was needing it less and less with each step as his body recovered.

"They know she's pregnant," he hissed, emerging outside. "Where is she?"

"Over there. Adams!" Priam shouted, pointing and helping a still-lurching Chief. "Come on out Adams, it's safe."

There was no response.

Another guard arrived to help Chief, taking his other side, but a few steps later he was pushing them off, his anger burning out the pain. They rounded the corner of the building. Sydney was nowhere in sight, but the unconscious form of one of Priam's guards was slumped against the side of the building.

"Shit."

Chief stepped forward, testing the air with his nose, letting his senses flow to the forefront. Almost immediately he picked up multiple trails he recognized. Sydney's was the strongest, but right there with it...

"Leighton," he hissed, following the scent, letting the change come over him.

He shifted as he ran, an ungainly, awkward gait made all the worse by the reshaping of his body. At one point he fell forward, but kept crawling, until he could get his legs under him, fully formed.

Fur sprouted and his face exploded in agony as it sprouted a muzzle, but that was the last of the change. He was in his animal form, and nearly five hundred pounds of furious dire wolf sprinted off into the woods, hot on the trail of his mate.

I'm coming, Sydney. Just hold on!

During his short-lived captivity, Chief had heard much of Leighton's plan. Of their intent to use her against him, to force him to return to Logan and the other rebels and betray them, at the threat of her life.

Chief couldn't let that happen. He would not let himself be forced to choose between his mate, or the cause. No, he would track Leighton and his men down, and rip them apart, one by one. Bathe the land in blood, if that's what it took.

But Chief *would* get his mate back. No matter the cost.

The one advantage he had was that he was the unencumbered one now. Free to shift, to run as fast as he could, without worry of abandoning Sydney. Leighton and his men had to take her with them. Not to mention they had to keep her in good condition. If she died, they had no leverage on Chief. None.

So he ran on, teeth bared, eyes tinged with red, uncaring about anything except for her. For the woman he cared for more than anything in the world. The mother of his child.

His mate.

Within minutes he could sense he was closing in on the rearguard. The scent was growing stronger by the second. Trees flashed past, and he leapt over rocks and cleared tiny valleys with massive leaps. Bushes pulled at his fur, but he kept going, not slowing for anything. Hair would regrow.

When he cleared the forest and ran into a meadow, he could see them up ahead. Five men and Sydney were nearly at the far edge. One of them had stuck behind, and was starting to change. They'd realized they weren't going to escape.

Putting on an extra burst of speed, Chief closed the distance, a blur as he flung his body at the rearguard, taking the man down with a snarl that split the air, echoing in the mountains for miles around.

It was time they paid for what they had done. He buried

his jaws in the man's neck and ripped at his torso with his paws.

No mercy.

CHAPTER 40

Molten iron filled his mouth, the metallic tang of metal as blood gushed from the neck wound. The man was screaming, the sounds quickly turning to a burble as blood filled his lungs. Chief opened wide, and in one brutal motion, ripped the rest of the man's neck out in a welter of gore and blood.

The fountain soaked the fur of his chest as he stood triumphantly over his first victim, eying the edge of the meadow where Leighton and the rest of his team were waiting. The other four shifters had paused and turned back. At some point, Leighton must have decided he was going to have to fight.

Now the leader stood, still in his human form, holding Sydney by the neck, while the rest of his men finished shifting into their wolf forms. Arrayed now in a line, they advanced, the four of them versus Chief. He growled and stepped down from the corpse of their comrade, opening his jaws so the chunk of his neck dropped to the ground, a visceral reminder of what he would do to any of them.

"You can't win!" Leighton shouted. "Turn back now, or they'll rip you to pieces."

Chief kept walking.

"Even if you beat them, I'll kill her before you get within ten steps of me," Leighton said, thrusting the hand around Sydney's neck forward, forcing her to move.

She cried out in pain, which only heightened the battle rage filling Chief. He was going to kill all of them, one by one. Leighton would be last, and he would be slow. The leader of the Tyrant-King's men would die a painful, lingering death.

"Whatever," Leighton said as the two sides continued to close. "Just rip him apart. Once he's dead we don't need the girl. We'll bury them together," he cackled.

Four shifters came at Chief, the wolves flowing over the meadow like a wave as they prepared to crash over him. He quickly surveyed his options, not liking any of them. He was outnumbered, and otherwise possessed no real advantages over the attackers. His wolf was bigger than any of them, but not by enough to matter.

Chief didn't care if he survived the oncoming fight, but he had to last long enough to get Sydney free. Which meant not necessarily killing all his opponents—just hurting them enough that they couldn't pursue her before she got back to safety.

Decision made, he focused on the largest, meanest looking of the four: an ugly white beast ever so slightly ahead of the rest of his companions, eager to be the first to fight. He smiled to himself as he aimed for the shifter to the *right* of that one. They wouldn't expect this at all. Not after what he'd done to their friend.

The five wolves raced across the meadow, accelerating to full speed moments before they collided. Chief crouched lower, making it look like he was readying himself to jump, to clear their lines, perhaps to go straight for Leighton.

The two outer wolves spread slightly wider, moving to counter that. Which created the opening Chief had been waiting for. He started to leap up, then flung himself to the side. He didn't go for the neck of his target. Not even the flank. He slipped past the side, jaws darting in just long enough to snatch at the white wolf's rear leg, ripping a chunk free as momentum carried him past.

The wolf howled in pain, clearly limping as he stood up, the lines now reformed on the other side. That trick would only work once, but Chief knew that he'd effectively reduced the odds by a quarter against him. For now.

"Chief, you don't have to do this. Let them take me!" Sydney shouted. "Find another way!"

He snarled, the only way he could think of to tell her to shut up. That simply wasn't happening.

Much to his dismay, however, the remaining three wolves didn't just dart back in to carry on the attack. Instead they slowed up, moving at the pace their wounded member could make. All of a sudden the odds had gone back to four against one. He was screwed.

Racing forward, he went on the attack, slamming full bore into the smallest of the wolves, using his superior size to send both of them spilling to the ground. The nearest wolf tore at his flank as he went by, ripping jagged holes with his claws as he passed, but Chief accepted that wound in exchange for the chance to badly hurt a second wolf.

Once more, blood filled his jaws as he dug deep into the belly. A second later, blinding pain filled his head as his victim's paw slammed into the side of his snout, ripping at the skin there, narrowly avoiding his eye.

Chief flung himself away, panting heavily by this point. The two unhurt wolves closed in fast, and he suffered another wound as one of them sunk its teeth deep into his hind leg.

Hurt badly, he hobbled away, putting some distance between them. This wasn't going well. Not at all. He was in real trouble now, and at risk of not saving his mate. He hadn't outright failed *yet*, but it was only a matter of time. They all knew that.

"You see!" Leighton called, arrogant in victory. "You can't win. You have *lost*. Just like your friends will lose. That pathetic rabble you call a rebellion. It's over. Accept it."

Chief was considering shifting back, bargaining with him. Her life, for his. He would gladly sacrifice himself if it meant that Sydney and the unborn child went free. It was unlikely that Leighton would agree, but the chances were better than those of him defeating all five remaining shifters alone. But before he could do that, a sound filled the meadow.

A howl.

Heads snapped back to the way they had come. A beautiful sable wolf strode from the forest, its pelt shiny and gorgeous in the mid-morning sunlight. Behind it, a trio of snow-white wolves stalked out of the trees, heads swinging left and right warily as they took in the situation.

Behind them came half a dozen more wolves of varying colors, spreading out, forming a line as they came. Chief paused. It was Priam and his guards. They had come after all. But whose side were they on? What was about to happen?

The black wolf, Priam, slowed as he passed the bloodied corpse of Chief's first victim. Chief steeled himself to fight, but the wolf, bigger even than Chief, simply came and stood at his side. The trio of white wolves followed. As did the rest, all of them moving to form a line at Chief's side that also served to block Leighton from the rest of his team.

Priam caught his attention, swinging the massive onyx-furred head over his shoulder toward Leighton. The meaning was clear.

We'll handle these men. Leighton is all yours.

Wasting no time, Chief started the shift back to his human form. It was time to end this. To secure the safety of his mate, and his child.

"Enough!" he shouted once he could speak. "Let her go, Leighton. It's over."

The enemy team leader laughed. "Just like that? Say 'oh you're free to go', shall I? Then what, do you want to circle up and sing a song? Hold hands around the campfire? I don't think so. Call off your dogs, or I'll snap her neck."

Sydney cried out in pain as Leighton tightened his grip.

CHAPTER 41

She struggled, trying to ignore the pain as steel fingers dug deep into her neck, threatening to crush bone. There was no doubt he was strong enough. Sydney had seen glimpses of Chief's strength. It was beyond human. Leighton would be no different.

The additional wolves were facing off against the rest of Leighton's team, but none of them were making a move. They all seemed to be waiting for a resolution between Chief and Leighton. A resolution that couldn't come if she was still in the way.

Chief isn't going to be able to do this for you, girl. You need to find a way to create an opening. Something he can exploit.

But how? She was just a human. There wasn't enough muscle in her body to break his grip. Not before he crippled or killed her. She briefly thought about trying to seduce Leighton, but realized that wouldn't work either. They knew she was carrying Chief's child. They'd said as much during their escape. About how they planned to use her to blackmail him into giving them information they needed.

She couldn't let that happen. Not now.

Think fast, girl. Real fast. How do you get yourself away from Leighton? What's he afraid of?

She looked at him up and down out of the corner of her eye. He was smartly dressed, shiny black combat boots, dark blue utility pants that, if anything, looked tailored, and a slim-fit combat vest over his dark-silver shirt. Every inch the jackboot thug that he was, immaculate on the battlefield. Like a true coward.

Sydney wiped a smile from her face as it came to her.

"Uh, guys," she said uneasily. "Can we hurry up and resolve this? This whole pregnancy thing is really messing with me. I'm going to be sick."

"Pathetic," Leighton sneered, while Chief looked alarmed, worried.

"You try growing another life inside of you, and complaining when it starts to push things out of both ends." She feigned a heave. "It's not as easy as you might think."

"What the? Ew," Leighton gagged.

"You don't say," she snapped. "But you dragging me through the forest, the blood, and the pressure of the baby are all sort of combining here. I'd really rather not projectile vomit. It's kind of embarrassing, you know?"

Leighton, like any arrogant male, was starting to look a little queasy. Sydney fell quiet for a bit. The key wasn't to push too hard. Just enough to make it appear real.

"It's over, Leighton," Chief called into the silence.

"You stay right there. I'll take her, and we'll go—"

"To a washroom? Seriously, I have to go so badly, I'm

not sure how much longer I can hold this." She shuffled slightly from side to side, sucking back some spit. Saving it.

"You *will* hold it." Leighton ordered, as if that mattered to a pregnant woman. Often the choice wasn't hers. Sydney was faking it, but he couldn't know that. Not for sure.

"I'll try. But I can't g—urpg." She started to act like her stomach was revolting, and then very carefully spilled all her spit in one giant retch as near to Leighton without getting it on him as possible.

"Fuck," she moaned, attempting to fall to her knees, ignoring the pain as he supported her by her neck.

"What the hell!" Leighton shouted, backing up furiously as she started to dry-heave some more.

Then all at once the pressure was gone. Sydney went prone as fast as possible, just barely reaching the ground before Chief went hurtling through the space she'd just occupied, taking Chief to the ground.

"How *dare* you threaten my mate," Chief snarled.

Turning just in time to see him unleash a vicious uppercut to Leighton's jaw, Sydney tried to clamp down on her fear. There were cuts up and down Chief's body, some of them even looking pretty bad.

The enemy leader roared in anger, snapping a kick up as Chief tried to gain the high ground. She winced from her position on the ground as Chief grunted and fell back in pain, holding his right shoulder.

Wolves snarled and yelped from behind her. Risking a quick look, she saw the newcomers fall over the rest of Leighton's team in a pile of teeth and claws. In very short order, the noises quieted and they dispersed, leaving the four wolves in heaps. None of them moved.

"Try to use my child against *me*!" Chief bellowed, and a moment later she heard something that sounded suspiciously like a bone snap.

"She's my woman!"

Snap.

"How dare you touch her!"

Snap.

"You." Snap. "Piece." Snap. "Of." Snap. "*Shit*."

By the time she turned her head around, Leighton was falling to the ground, his arms and legs bent out of shape, his nose gushing blood, clearly broken, jaw hanging loose, caved in on one side.

"I will protect her," Chief hissed. "I will protect both of them. And you will never threaten them again."

Sydney closed her eyes, clamping her hands over her ears as Chief went for Leighton's neck. The next thing she knew, someone was shaking her gently.

"Syd. Syd."

Her eyes flew open, finding Chief's blue eyes staring down at her in concern. "Are you okay?"

"Fine," she said. "I'm fine. Are you?"

"I'm not gonna die," he said with a wince. "But there's something I need to tell you."

She nodded.

"I love you."

Reaching up with one hand, she stroked his face, taking it all in.

"I know," she said, pulling him down for a kiss. "I love you too."

CHAPTER 42

His first priority was to get them back to the village. Priam had detailed some of his men to stay behind, while the rest of them acted as an escort, patrolling the woods on either side of them as they went, ensuring nothing else happened. Very little was said until they reached the Council building, and the quarters assigned to them below.

"Your men?" Chief asked as he settled Sydney down gently into a chair, despite her constant assurances that she was okay. He didn't care, this was his fault, and he was going to treat her as cautiously as he wanted to for now, until he was assured they hadn't hurt her at all.

"They're fine," Priam said from the door. "A few cuts here or there, but none of them will admit to anything. They don't want to be the one that took the stupid injury when we outnumbered them that badly."

Chief chuckled, knowing exactly what Priam meant, but then he sobered quickly.

"Thank you," he said, looking at the Alpha with earnest.

"But I have to wonder. *Why*? This wasn't your fight. You didn't need to get involved in the middle of it."

"Except I did," Priam said heavily. "Not by choice. But out of obligation."

Chief sat down next to Sydney, putting one arm around her protectively. "What do you mean?"

"I am the Alpha here, Chief. This is *my* pack. They respect my rules, and they respect me as a ruler, because I treat everyone the same. If they follow the rules, no problems. If they break them, everyone gets the same treatment, from me on down."

Nodding, Chief was starting to understand. "Leighton and his men broke the rules."

"Precisely. They showed no respect to what we've built here. No respect to our rules. No respect to me. I could not let that stand. They needed to be shown the error of their ways. You understand."

"I do," Chief said. "I know you didn't do it for my sake, but I'm still grateful to you, for coming to my aid."

"As am I," Sydney said, speaking up. "Thank you, for risking your lives for me. And I'm sorry that you had to. We should have been more careful to prevent this sort of thing from happening."

Priam snorted. "I don't side with you, nor do I side against you. But I think we both know that Leighton had no intention of obeying my rules. He was going to go after you no matter what. We all know his type."

Chief inclined his head in agreement, trying to mask the disappointment at Priam's other words. The ones that told Chief his mission here had been a failure.

Priam must have noticed anyway. "You don't like what I have to say."

"It's not that I don't understand," Chief said. "I do. I just had hoped you would see that we're trying to do the right thing here."

"I do, Chief. I do see. You're trying to do the right thing for you. But I too am trying to do the right thing, for my people. Which isn't necessarily the same. That is why I, and the Council, will not declare our support for you."

"I understand," Chief said. "Thank you for listening to us."

What were they going to do now? Without the support from the Pacific, it was unlikely that others would choose to side with them either. Their rebellion would be tough.

Still, they could do it. They *had* to do it, in fact. Giving up just wasn't an option for them, not after all they've already done. The Tyrant-King Laurien *had* to be brought down. For their safety, and for the safety of others.

His mind immediately strayed to Sydney, and he rested a hand on her stomach. Keeping her safe was his top priority. Maybe he could find a solution where she stayed with Priam, out of harm's way. Where she could be well taken care of until the baby came. It would mean a distance between them, but it would be for the best.

"Don't even think it," Sydney hissed abruptly at his side.

"Think what?"

"I am *not* staying here. I can see that look in your eye. I feel your hand on my stomach," she told him when he went wide-eyed in surprise. "I'm figuring you out now. You would do anything to keep me safe."

"I would."

"Well, I'm going to be safest near you. So get that idea out of your head. Just because they won't fight doesn't mean you get to leave me behind."

Before Chief could reply, Priam cleared his throat.

"I did not say none of us will fight."

Chief frowned. "I'm pretty sure that's what you said."

"No." Priam smiled. "I said I and the Council will not declare our support for you. The Pacific will not side with you. I cannot side with you. However, there are many here who *do* wish to help you. Adams!" he barked.

The door opened, and the guard came in. "Sir," he said sharply.

"What is the latest count?" Priam inquired lightly.

Chief looked back and forth, tamping down his hope. Did this mean what he thought it meant?

"Forty-three," Adams said tightly. "But we're still waiting on decisions from others. I feel confident in saying that fifty is not an unreasonable number."

Chief gaped. *Fifty*? With over four dozen more shifters added to the cause, the rebellion would be well over three-quarters of a hundred. There was no doubt in his mind that once word of this got around, others would come as well. House Canis had an enclave in most major cities. Often no more than half a dozen, many of them older, but still. Enough would come.

They would have the support they needed.

"Thank you," he breathed, not trusting his own voice. "Thank you."

Sydney took his hand and squeezed it. "Yes, thank you. With your support, I know the chances of this big idiot coming back to me every time will be much higher. I kind of like him."

Priam smiled. "Yes, we can tell. You two make an excellent pairing."

Sydney leaned into him. "I think so too."

CHAPTER 43

"Did you mean that?" Chief asked, several hours into the journey back home.

"Mean what?" She looked over at him, pulling herself out of her blank stare at the road winding through the mountains in front of them.

"About me. Us. That you think we make a good, uh, pair."

Instead of replying right away, she gave it some thought. Some *more* thought. She'd been up late, thinking about a different decision. That one had required much more thought than this, but she wanted to give it proper thought.

Her and Chief. Together. An item. No, not an item; that implied too much casualness. They weren't in college anymore. Both of them were grown adults, leading their own lives, talking about bringing them together as one. This was far more serious than simply dating.

Sydney blinked in surprise as the expected panic attack at the subject didn't materialize. Every time before, she'd freaked out internally at the idea of being with Chief in a serious manner. Yet now…

"Yes, I meant it," she said, realizing that was all the sign she needed. When thinking about it brought a smile to her face, and not a spike in her heart combined with shortness of breath while she tried not to panic, the answer was clear.

Reaching across the center console, she laid her hand out, palm up. Chief glanced down, saw it, and with a smile took her hand in his.

"This has to have been the weirdest trip I've ever taken in my life," she said into the silence that followed, basking in the strength of his grip as he held her tight. Protective. Safe.

"I think I can understand that," Chief said with a chuckle, looking over his shoulder for a moment.

"I thought I was going on a babymoon. Turns out I'm actually helping you recruit people to fight in a war." Sydney shook her head. "No, not just people. *Wolf* shifters. People who can turn into fantastic and terrifying animals. Which is also what my child is going to be. My child. A wolf shifter. That one is going to take some getting used to, I'm not going to lie to you, Chief. That won't be an overnight thing."

She was smiling as she spoke, even if it was the truth. Sydney had had long enough to accept it that she no longer freaked out about it. Coming to terms with it as the new normal, however, would take longer.

"I understand." There was a tenseness to his voice, though he tried hard to hide it.

Sydney smiled wider, knowing full well what it was

about. "I wanted to speak with you about that as well," she said softly.

"About what?"

"Our child. And, um, the offer you made." She was biting her lip, nervous despite being fairly positive she knew the answer.

"What offer?" Chief's eyes were flicking back and forth between her and the road.

"Um, you know. The one about you. Me. The baby. Um. Being a, uh, you know." She was blowing it, her nerves getting the better of her.

"A family?" Chief supplied softly, meeting her eyes for a long moment before watching the road again. "That offer?"

"Yeah," she said with a nervous laugh. "That one. Um. If it's still on the table…"

"It is," Chief said, though that was all he gave her.

"You're going to make me say it, aren't you?" she asked weakly.

"Yup."

"Fine. If you're still okay with it, I think I'd like to keep the child. With us. Together. Like a family."

Chief smiled, squeezing her hand. "I would love that, Sydney. As much as I love you."

"Really?"

"Yes. Yes so much yes. Absolutely." He grinned and suddenly blasted on the horn, rolling down the window and sticking his other hand out, waving it around.

"What are you doing?!" she yelped as he stole a hand back to honk the horn some more and steer with it.

Behind them came a caravan of trucks and SUVs.

Moments later, all of them started doing the same, honking and waving their arms.

"They can't possibly know what this is all about, can they?" Sydney asked in astonishment.

Chief just winked at her.

"You shifters are *weird*," she said.

Chief laughed, then sobered, rolling up the window. "Thank you," he said quietly. "For pushing out of your comfort zone."

Sydney blushed. "Thank you for giving me the push I needed, and being there to catch me when I fall. Which I'm sure I'll do lots of, raising our child."

"We'll do it together," Chief told her, finding her hand again and squeezing it. "I promise. I have no experience being a father either. But together, we'll be the best parents our son could ask for."

Frowning, she rested one hand on her belly. "Or daughter."

"Right," Chief said, nodding. "But our son will be well loved."

"Or our *daughter*."

Chief scratched his chin. "Are you having twins?"

"I don't think so," she said, confused. "I'm just telling you not to get your hopes up."

Chief grinned. "I'm not. But shifter genes rarely produce first born females. So, if you want a daughter, we're going to have to have another one."

"Oh," she said in a very small voice. "Oh my."

Chief winked.

CHAPTER 44

They pulled up the laneway to the house, turning off the road onto the dirt roadway.

Sydney was bouncing in her seat, eager to get out and stretch. The drive home had been done in a much shorter time than the drive out, and she was sick and tired of being cramped.

"You don't think adding another fifteen or so vehicles to the property is going to be, oh I dunno, a little suspicious to anyone?" she asked. "I thought you guys were trying to keep a low profile out here?"

She'd had a *lot* of questions on the way home, and Chief had clued her in to everything going on with the conflict, and how this was their hideout, their base, that they were working to keep secret at all costs.

"The secret won't last much longer," Chief told her. "Plus, for all we know, they already have the location. I still find it hard to believe Leighton just randomly came across us while we were driving, but I didn't get a chance to question him. We'll keep them hidden from the road, but other than that, better to have transportation than not."

Sydney couldn't find fault with that logic.

"Besides, with Adams bringing nearly sixty shifters with him, well, I doubt Laurien would strike us here. It would take something big for him to make that sort of move."

"If you're certain. I'm just glad to be back."

Chief pulled the truck to a halt and she was hopping out before it had fully come turned off, arms above her head, stretching with a loud groan as muscles, joints, ligaments and tendons all popped, creaked or otherwise did things they hadn't been able to do for the last six hours. It was glorious.

"You're back!"

She turned as Logan came out from the main building, arms wide.

"We are," she said with a smile. "And we didn't come alone."

"Oh?' Logan turned as the first of the Pacific trucks pulled up the laneway behind them, the start of a procession of seventeen different vehicles that had made the trek cross-country with them. It was an impressive show as they all pulled up and huge shifters began exiting, milling around, uncertain of what to do now.

"You did it," Logan said, looking surprised. "They came."

"Some of them," she said as Chief walked around the front of their vehicle. "Not all. The Pacific is a lot bigger than anyone suspected. But these ones came, volunteers all."

"Good work," Logan said, beaming. "Bloody good work, both of you."

He whistled sharply, summoning some of the other rebels to come out and assist in getting everyone squared away. Sydney did not envy them that job at all.

"Thank you," Logan said, sweeping her and Chief up into a hug. "Both of you." He stepped back, eying the two of them. "You two are holding hands."

Sydney looked down. She hadn't even realized it, so natural had it become on their trek back. It just felt normal now, she barely thought about it.

"Uh, I guess we are," she said with a shrug, not letting go of Chief. "Sorry to break your heart."

Logan was already opening his mouth to respond, but her last words stole whatever he was about to say.

"Break my..." he repeated quietly, then laughed loudly. "That's great. I suspect Chief is going to find himself...oh, I won't ruin the surprise. But seriously, I'm happy for you two. That's wonderful. Are you...staying around?" he asked.

"I'm going to live at my place. There's *way* too much testosterone here."

"Tell me about it," another female voice muttered, emerging from the big farmhouse.

Sydney eyed the brunette. She looked vaguely familiar, but it wasn't someone she'd met yet.

"This is Alison," Logan said, introducing them. "She's Lucien's mate. He's the ugly dork organizing this mob."

Alison elbowed Logan as she came by. "Nice to meet you."

"Sydney," she said, introducing herself and returning the hug.

"You're staying, right? Nearby, at least? Please? I need more women here."

"I live next door. You're welcome to come visit anytime," Sydney said. "And I'm sure I'll be here more often. What with this one wanting to see us all the time."

Alison frowned, pushing back her long hair. "Us?"

Sydney moved one hand to her stomach. "Yeah."

Alison's eyes went wide. "Oh my goodness! You're? You two? That's so great! Come on, let's go inside, I'm gonna have some wine, you get water. Tell me *all* about it."

She grabbed Sydney by the wrist and started dragging her along. Looking over her shoulder at Chief, she saw he was just smiling.

"Go on, I have work to do out here anyway," he urged, making a shooing motion with his hands.

Logan was just grinning as she went passed.

"Welcome to the family," he told her.

Sydney let herself be dragged along in a bit of a daze as she went.

Welcome to the family.

Logan had said it so offhandedly, but to her, it meant so much more. She and Chief were their own little family. Now it seemed she'd gained another one, a much more extended family.

And the truth about it, she thought, grinning ear to ear as Alison dragged her inside for girl talk.

The truth was, she was perfectly okay with it. Sydney had found her place.

She'd found her home.

ABOUT THE AUTHOR

Riley Storm

Riley is one of those early-morning people you love to hate, because she swears she doesn't need caffeine, even though the coffee-maker is connected to her smartphone. She lives in a three-story townhouse by the good graces of a tabby-cat who rules the house, the couch, the table, well, basically everywhere. When she's not groveling for forgiveness for neglecting to pet her kitty enough, Riley is strapped in to her writing chair coming up with crazy worlds where she can make her own decisions of when feeding time is and how much coffee can be drank without her friends—of which she has three—holding yet another intervention that they threaten to post on the internet.

Made in the USA
Lexington, KY
03 September 2019